Winter in Wartime

Winter in Wartime

Jan Terlouw

McGraw-Hill Book Company
New York   St. Louis   San Francisco

Library of Congress Cataloging in Publication Data

Terlouw, Jan.
    Winter in wartime.

    Translation of Oorlogswinter.
    SUMMARY: Michiel and his village join the resistance
in German-occupied Holland during World War II.
    [1. Netherlands—History—German occupation, 1940–
1945—Fiction. 2. World War, 1939–1945—Underground
movements—Netherlands—Fiction] I. Title.
PZ7.T268Wi3   [Fic]   75-41345
ISBN 0-07-063504-8 Lib. bdg.

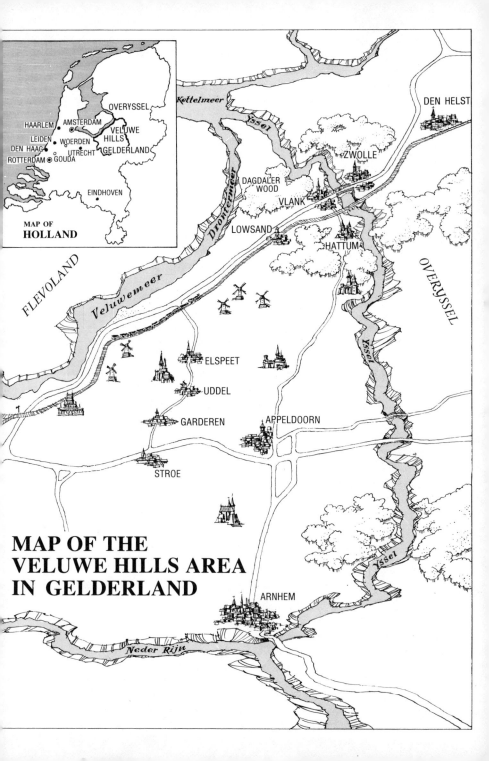

MAP OF
HOLLAND

OVERYSSEL
AMSTERDAM
HAARLEM
VELUWE
LEIDEN
HILLS
WOERDEN
DEN HAAG
UTRECHT
GELDERLAND
ROTTERDAM
GOUDA

EINDHOVEN

Kettelmeer

DEN HELST

Yssel

ZWOLLE

DAGDALER
WOOD

VLANK

FLEVOLAND

Dronten-meer

LOWSAND

HATTUM

OVERYSSEL

Veluwemeer

Yssel

ELSPEET

UDDEL

GARDEREN

APPELDOORN

STROE

MAP OF THE
VELUWE HILLS AREA
IN GELDERLAND

Yssel

ARNHEM

Neder Rijn

Winter in Wartime

Chapter 1

It was dark.

Step by step, one hand groping in front of him, Michiel edged his way along the rough bicycle path that ran parallel to the cart track. In his other hand he carried a cotton bag containing two bottles of milk. "New moon and heavy clouds," he muttered. "Van Ommen's farm should be around here somewhere." He peered to the right, straining his eyes, but could see nothing at all. Next time I'll refuse to go if they don't give me the lantern, he thought. Erica should make sure she's at home by half past seven! I can't manage this way.

How right he was! His cotton bag bumped against one of the little posts which had been placed at

1

intervals to prevent the farm wagons from driving on
to the bicycle path. "Damn!" Carefully, he felt with
his hand. Wet! One of the bottles had broken. "What
a shame! All that precious milk." Irritated, he groped
his way forward with even more caution. It really was
impossible to see much in this light. He was no more
than seven hundred yards from home and knew every
stone of the way, yet he would still be lucky to be in
before eight o'clock.

Wait, what was that? He saw the faintest trickle of
light. Ah, good! Bogard's house! They weren't being
very careful about the blackout, even though they had
only one candle to worry about. Well, there were no
more posts now as far as the main road. He knew that
for sure. Once on the road, everything would be
easier to find. There were more houses, for one thing,
which somehow seemed to take away from the darkness a little.

Milk dropped into one of his clogs. He tried to peer
ahead. Anyone on the road? Not very likely at this
time of night. It was nearly eight o'clock when the
curfew began and everyone had to be off the streets.
He felt the pavement under his feet. At last, the road!
Turn right, now, and watch out for the ditch. As he
had expected, he could now move ahead more easily.
Very dimly he could make out the outlines of the
houses—the de Ruiter's, the Zomer's, the smithy, the
little Green Cross social-services building—he was
almost home.

Without warning, a flashlight blazed straight into
his eyes. He stood still, petrified.

"It's after eight," said a voice in broken Dutch. "You're under arrest. What's that you've got there? A hand grenade?"

"Put that flash away, Dirk," Michiel said. "Phew! What a fright you gave me." Their neighbor's son, Dirk, was fond of practical jokes, and at twenty-one was scared of nothing, not even of the devil himself.

"A bit of a scare will harden your nerves. It really is after eight. Any German can come along and shoot you—you're a threat to the great German Empire. *Heil Hitler!*"

"Sh! You shouldn't go shouting that name around the place."

"Why not?" said Dirk breezily. "Our darling occupying forces love to hear it."

Walking by Michiel's side, Dirk kept his hand over the beam, so that only a sliver of light was visible. It seemed like daylight to Michiel, as he could even see the side of the road.

"Where did you get that flash? And the batteries?"

"Pinched them from the Boche."

"Go on!" said Michiel, incredulous.

"It's true. We've got two officers at home, don't forget. This week, one of them—you know, the fat one—had a carton of some ten of these flashlights in his room. Well, it's our room, isn't it? So, what's his is ours, if you see what I mean. So I stole one."

"You go into their room!"

"Yes, of course. I take stock every day when they're out—there's no danger. The only one I have to be careful of is my father, he's timid as a mouse. If he knew I had this lamp, he wouldn't sleep tonight. But then he doesn't sleep anyway, so what does it matter? Can you find your way now?"

"Yes, thanks. Love to the Germans!"

Michiel's clogs crunched over the gravel in the front garden. He was glad Dirk had not noticed the broken bottle. He would certainly have pulled his leg about it.

————

Inside the house, the flame of the carbide lamp was still bright. It was always like that early in the evening, just after his father had filled it. Filling it was a nasty job, because of the unpleasant smell. But once the iron container was closed and the flame burning, the smell disappeared. It was almost as good as electric light. Unfortunately, it became weaker and weaker, until there was only a tiny blue flame—just enough light to keep one from falling over every chair in the room.

Michiel had discovered eighteen old books by Jules Verne that he was longing to read in his father's bookcase. But during the day, when there was enough light, there was no time. At night there was time but no light. Early in the evening he could read at several yards' distance from the lamp. Later, he could decipher the words only by holding the book right up to the flame. This was unfair to everyone else—especially if there were guests present, as there usually were.

Tonight the room was crowded. Apart from his mother and father, his sister Erica, and his six-year-old brother Jochem, Michiel counted about ten other people. The only one he recognized was his Uncle Ben. His mother introduced the others. One was a very old lady who said she was Aunty Gerty and who even wanted to kiss him—he had never heard of her. His mother explained that she was a remote cousin on the paternal side, and that his father had not seen her for twenty years. Two other ladies he had never seen before exclaimed at how tall he had grown; an elderly, cocksure gentleman addressed him as "sonny" even though Michiel was almost sixteen. They all seemed to know exactly who *he* was.

"They've done their homework well," Michiel muttered to himself.

They had all come from the west of the country, driven toward the north and east in search of food. It was the beginning of winter 1944, and wartime. No food was to be had in the cities and as there was no transport, they had to walk. Often they traveled tens, sometimes hundreds, of miles with little carts or baby carriages, or on bicycles without tires, and on other odd contraptions. Because of the eight o'clock curfew, it was essential to have acquaintances who lived along the way. Michiel's parents had no idea that they knew so many people, or, rather, that so many people knew them.

Night after night, from seven o'clock onward, the doorbell rang constantly and some person stood on the step calling out brightly, "Hello there! How are you all? Don't you recognize me? Annie from The Hague. I've thought about you all so often." It might have been funny had it not been so tragic. Annie was someone Michiel's parents had met just once at the house of a mutual acquaintance. But as soon as it dawned on you that Annie was badly undernourished, that she was on the last reserves of her energy, that she had walked the whole way from The Hague in old slippers—all to get a few pounds of potatoes for her daughter's children—then you said, "Of course! Do come in! How are you, Aunt Annie—if I may call you that?" She was handed a cup of pea soup, given a place near the carbide lamp, and a bed or a mattress for the night on the floor.

As soon as Michiel had greeted them all, he signaled to his mother to go with him to the kitchen. At such times the pinchcat came in handy. This was a sort of bicycle electric generator, which gave off a small flash of light so long as you kept moving the knob up and down with your thumb; but your thumb got tired after a while.

"I'm sorry, Mother, but I broke one bottle on my way home."

"Oh! How could you be so careless?" his mother exclaimed. "You clumsy boy!"

Michiel stopped working the pinchcat and pushed aside the curtains to show her the pitch black outside.

"There was no moon and I had no flash," he said apologetically. He pulled the curtains to, and started the pinchcat again with his thumb so that they could see what they were doing.

"I'm sorry, Michiel," she said, and smoothed his hair by way of apology. "I didn't mean to say that. You couldn't help it, of course. I was only thinking of all these people in the room who would like coffee."

Coffee was in fact nothing more than some substitute or other with a brown color. The hot milk made it more or less drinkable.

"I can't go again," Michiel said, "it's after eight. If you hold the light, I'll get rid of the splinters."

"Let's leave that till tomorrow. Give me the other bottle. . . . Thanks. How did it happen?"

"I knocked into a little post near Van Ommen's farmhouse. Shall I pour the other bottle of milk into the saucepan?"

"Let me do it."

Michiel started the pinchcat again and a moment later they went back into the living room, where the milk was warmed on the stove. The stove was heated with bits of wood for they had long ago run out of coal.

When the coffee was finished the guests began talking about life in the big towns. Hunger, cold, and fear of arrest were the main subjects. Everything was scarce, everything uncertain. Everybody had some story or other about families forced to go into hiding, or a friend who had been sent to a concentration camp, or a house destroyed by a bomb. Then they discussed the war rumors: the American, General Patton, was doing very well on the western front, the Germans had suffered heavy losses on the Russian front—or so it was said.

Then came the jokes about the war. Anton Mussert, leader of the Dutch National Socialist Party, was said to have married his aunt. Mr. Van der Heiden told about a film in which Mussert had appeared.

Somebody in the front had called out, "Anton, An-ton!" and a voice at the back had replied, "Yes, my dear aunt." Michiel, his parents, and the others laughed a good deal at these stories.

Uncle Ben said, "Ever hear about the bet between Goering, Goebbels, and Hitler as to who could stay in a skunk hole the longest? Goering tried first and was out in quarter of an hour, quite sick. Then Goebbels tried and lasted half an hour. Finally Hitler went in—and the skunks came out at once!"

Such simple jokes were enough to make the whole company, overstrained as they were with anxiety and misery, roar with laughter.

The carbide lamp was nearly dead. Carrying odd bits of candle, everyone shuffled to bed or to a mattress on the floor. Michiel checked the supply of kindlings for lighting the stove in the morning, while his mother worked the pinchcat. Then he felt his way upstairs, undressed, and went to bed. Far away he could hear the sound of an airplane. "Rinus de Raadt," Michiel muttered. "I hope he doesn't come this way."

Rinus de Raadt was the local shoemaker's son. At the beginning of the war he had managed to get to England. Michiel's father said he had become a pilot there. That was why everybody in the village always said, "Here comes Rinus de Raadt," whenever they heard a plane.

Michiel drifted into sleep and was no longer con-scious of the one thousand, six hundred, and eleventh night of the German occupation.

Chapter 2

When the German Army, ordered by Adolf Hitler, invaded Holland and Belgium on the tenth of May 1940 Michiel was eleven years old. He still remembered the radio pouring out news of paratroopers dropping on the "Ypenburg airport, repeat Ypenburg, and Waalhaven, repeat Waalhaven." All day long, soldiers on horseback passed through the village. They joked with the girls and looked very brave. Michiel decided for himself that war was an exciting business and he hoped it would last for a long time.

He soon had good reason to change his mind. The first doubts came after five days when the Dutch Army capitulated. His father's face had turned white when the news came over the radio and his mother wept. Then there was the concern for the fourteen boys from the village who were in the army.

News came in from eight of them that they were all right. Some days later it was reported that three others were safe; but from the last three—Gerrit, the baker's son, Hendrik Bosser, a farmer's son, and their gardener's son, called Whitey on account of his blond hair—there was no news. Michiel still remembered how he sat on the wheelbarrow, watching Whitey's father working in the garden. He said nothing, just worked steadily. He was still working steadily a week later, after the news that Gerrit and Hendrik were safe. Gerrit had been taken prisoner and subsequently released. His round face shone with pleasure as he told how a German officer had pointed at the freckles that covered his face from forehead to chin. "They're the rusty ends of my iron nerves," he had retorted. That one little bit of defiance had made Gerrit feel that they had not lost the war, after all.

Hendrik Bosser had simply not thought of sending a letter home to say he was all right.

Whitey had been buried at the Grebbeberg. Whitey's father continued to weed the garden of Michiel's father, Mayor Van Beusekom, and said nothing.

Yes, by then Michiel had realized that his wish was a stupid one and that it would have been *better if the war had ended there and then. But the war had gone on and on. Four years and five months it was, since that tenth of May 1940. It was true that last June the British and Americans had landed in France, driven the Germans back, and even liberated the south of the country, but they had not yet crossed the rivers. They had tried near Arnhem, but sadly, the battle of Arnhem was won by the Germans. And now winter had come again, a pitch-black winter. The Germans knew full well that they were losing and that was why they were now creating havoc everywhere. Everything edible was seized and sent to Germany. This was why the big cities were starving. In the air the Germans were below strength. The British and American fighters were buzzing around destroying every means of transport they could spot. This forced the Germans to do their transporting at night, when it was dark, which was not so easy.*

The village of Vlank, where Michiel's father was Mayor, lay in the north part of the Veluwe, near Zwolle. The river Yssel divided Vlank and Zwolle. There were two bridges across the river, one for trains and the other for traffic. The Allied forces were trying to destroy them by constant bombardment. If they succeeded, this would greatly hinder the German traffic. But these bridges also gave the Germans the opportunity to stop people and check their papers. Young men were arrested there and sent to Germany to work in the munition factories. The Germans could also pick out people in hiding, who had false identification cards. The bridges were natural traps.

And that was why so many people stopped at Vlank: to find out how strict the control was at the bridges. It was known that the Mayor was no friend of the Germans. So there was a lot of coming and going at the Van Beusekoms' house.

The morning after the night of the broken milk bottle, Michiel got up at half past seven. He expected to be the first, but no, Uncle Ben was already lighting the stove. Uncle Ben was not a real uncle. Erica, Jochem, and Michiel called him that because he came so often. He usually stayed a few days. They didn't mind him, because he always brought something into the house, even half an ounce of tea, and a real cigar for their father.

"Good morning, Uncle Ben."

"Hello, Michiel. I need your help, boy. I must get half, or, rather, a whole sack of potatoes. Do you know where I could go?"

"We could try Van de Bos. His farm is rather a long way, nearly half an hour by bicycle from here. But he's well off the main road and doesn't have many visitors. I can come with you if you like."

"Fine!"

The room was warming up nicely as the stove blazed away. Michiel looked at it suspiciously. The wet wood they normally used wouldn't be burning that well. He lifted the lid of the old oak chest. It was empty. Uncle Ben had taken the sticks of "wood-for-desperate-moments."

"Hey, did you take those sticks?" Michiel asked sharply.

"Yes, so what?"

"You know Mother is sometimes desperate when the stove goes out just before the meal is ready. That's what those sticks are for. We call them 'wood-for-desperate-moments.' Dad and I chop them very thin and dry them behind the stove."

Uncle Ben looked guilty. "I'll replace them personally," he said.

Michiel nodded. It'll take you more than an hour, he thought, but he said nothing. He did not offer to do it himself. If you make such a mistake, you have to pay for it, he thought.

Gradually the guests appeared. They were given two pieces of bread soaked in ersatz coffee and a bowl of some kind of porridge. They thanked Mrs. Van Beusekom for her kindness and went on their way; some to the north, to get a peck of rye or a sack of potatoes; some to the west and back home, where their starving families waited.

When the family had had their breakfast, Uncle Ben asked Michiel to show him the way to the Van de Bos farm. Michiel looked meaningfully at the old oak chest and said he had to go to the Wessels with two rabbits. Uncle Ben shamefacedly looked for the axe and went to the chopping block behind the barn. Michiel fed his thirty rabbits, chose two, weighed them and went to the Wessels, quite determined to ask fifty guilders for them.

Michiel had not been to school for months. He was in the fourth form of the secondary school in Zwolle, but there was no way of getting there. The first day after the summer holiday, he had tried by train. That had been some journey. First an airplane appeared. The train stopped, the passengers got out and ran into the fields as the British fighter swept very low over their heads. But the pilot was not after the people, he was looking for any means of transport the Germans might use. Once the passengers were far enough away, the fighter dived down at the engine and riddled it with bullets.

That was the end of the journeys to school. Michiel could not go by bicycle, either. There were no rubber tires, and to go on wooden ones was simply not possible. Moreover, Michiel's parents thought any form of travel too dangerous and kept him at home. It was one of the few things that they decided for him; for the rest he was now independent. That was the influence of the war. He would wander about here and there and come back with bacon, butter, and eggs. He worked at farmhouses and conducted his own little trade. He repaired wheelbarrows, bicycles, and knapsacks for passersby. He knew the hiding places of several Jewish people. He knew who had a hidden wireless and he knew that Dirk was a member of the resistance. His knowing all this didn't matter, as Michiel was reserved by nature and knew how to keep his own counsel.

On his return from the Wessels, where he had earned seventy guilders, he met Dirk at the gate.

"'Morning."

"Can I talk to you privately?" Dirk asked.

"Come along to the barn. What's the matter?"

Dirk said nothing till they were right inside. "Nobody can hear us?" he asked.

"Good heavens, no. There's nobody here, it's quite safe. By the way, you can trust everyone in our house."

Dirk was more serious than usual. "Swear that you won't tell anybody."

"I swear," Michiel said.

"Tonight three of us are going to raid the distribution office at Lowsand."

Lowsand was a village five miles from Vlank. Michiel felt a queer sensation in his stomach, but his face showed nothing.

"What for?"

"It's like this," Dirk said. "There are many people hidden in the neighborhood and they don't get ration cards for bread, sugar, tobacco, or suchlike."

It was impossible to buy anything without these cards.

"I see," said Michiel.

"Well," Dirk said, "we're going to raid the distribution office, take the ration cards, and give them to people in hiding."

"How are you going to open the safe?"

"I am sure Mr. Van Willigenburg will open it for me."

"Who is he?"

"The director. He's anti-German and I know he will be there tonight. We'll persuade him to open it and give us all the new cards. I don't think he'll give us too much trouble."

"Who are we?"

"Never mind." Of course, Dirk could not mention names.

Michiel grinned. "Why are you telling me all this?"

"Look, Michiel, here is a letter. If anything goes wrong, give it to Bertus Van Gelder. That's all. O.K.?"

"Of course. But do you think things *will* go wrong?"

"No, but you can never be sure. Have you somewhere you can hide it?"

"Yes, give it to me."

Dirk had taken an envelope from under his shirt. It was sealed and had no name or address.

"Where are you going to hide it?"

"Never mind."

It was Dirk's turn to grin.

"Tomorrow I'll come and get it," he said.

"Don't get caught, Dirk."

"I won't. Take good care of the letter. Be seeing you."

"'Bye."

He left the barn, whistling. Michiel waited behind

and opened a door to the hen house. He took out the straw from the fourth hutch where the wooden bottom was loose. He lifted it and placed the letter underneath. Then he put everything in order again. Nobody would find it there. He went up to his bedroom and wrote in pencil "4h" on the wooden partition of his bed. Not that he was likely to forget it, but you never knew.

Well now, what next? Ah yes, to Mr. Van de Bos with Uncle Ben. He went downstairs and met Uncle Ben, who had his arms full of sticks on his way to the living room.

With a twinkle in his eye, Uncle Ben asked, "Is the master content?"

"First-class work," Michiel said. "Shall we go? I'm sure Father won't mind you borrowing his bike."

"I've already asked him and it's all right," Uncle Ben said. "Have *you* got a vehicle of sorts?"

"One rubber and one wooden tire," Michiel replied cheerfully. "It gives you a pleasant sort of bump."

"Well, let's go then."

On the road, Uncle Ben told him about the resistance movement in Utrecht. "Our most important task is to organize ways of escape," he said.

"Escape from prison? Is that possible?"

"No, not from prison, although they've done some brave things in that line. I mean escape from the country. Nearly every day British and American pilots are shot down. If the pilots can reach the ground safely, they hide and try to get into contact with the resistance movement. Then we try to get them back to England, sometimes on board a ship, sailing by night, sometimes via Spain."

A fighter, flying very low overhead, made conversation impossible for a moment. When it had passed, Uncle Ben continued, "There are some groups in the resistance who kill off German officers, but I think it's very unwise. The only result is that the Boche take reprisal victims and shoot them."

Michiel nodded. Not so long ago one of his father's colleagues had been murdered in just such a manner.

"Do they often manage to get the pilots out of the country?" he asked.

"Unfortunately they are often caught on their way back and are sent to prisoner-of-war camps. But if a Dutchman is caught helping them, he is shot after they torture him until he has given away all the names and addresses of his contacts. That's why we try to organize things so that people helping don't know names and addresses."

"Isn't what you do terribly dangerous?"

"Oh no, not really. My job is to get false passports and other papers. I know a few people in hiding who are experts in the field. I reckon they ought to become forgers after the war. They could make a fortune." Uncle Ben grinned.

The noise from Michiel's wooden wheel made conversation barely possible. By now they had turned to the right and were on a sandy track with a narrow, hardened path for bicycles. They had to ride in single file. As Michiel knew the way, he went in front.

The farmer was prepared to sell Uncle Ben half a sack of rye at the reasonable price of thirty cents a kilo. The farmers in that part of the country were not profiteers. Strictly speaking, they were not allowed to sell to a private person, but were supposed to hand over their entire harvest to the German-controlled farmers' organization. Mr. Van de Bos looked suspiciously at Uncle Ben, but since Michiel was the son of the Mayor, who was absolutely trustworthy, he did not hesitate.

"Nice people, these farmers," Uncle Ben remarked on the way back.

"Oh yes, you think they're all right now, don't you? But before the war you townspeople always looked down on them. You treated them like dirt."

"Not me. I always thought farmers important."

It was a quiet day. Far away, near the river, shooting could be heard, but that was nothing unusual and no one paid any attention.

Back home again, Michiel tended to the hens and rabbits, took a letter from his father to one of the aldermen because the telephones no longer worked, and helped someone with a broken-down cart full of potatoes. As he made himself useful, at the back of his mind was the thought, I wish it were tomorrow. It was not that Dirk's plan was all that dangerous, such attacks happened quite often, but even so . . .

Evening fell and the house gradually filled up with the usual guests. Between nine and ten o'clock the continuous noise of airplanes droned overhead. They were American bombers on their way to Germany.

"That means the lives of hundreds of civilians," Mrs. Van Beusekom sighed, but her remark failed to impress any of her family.

"It serves them right," the Mayor said. "They started this horrible war. They were the first to drop bombs on defenseless cities—Warsaw, Rotterdam. Tit for tat's fair play."

"Yes, but the little girl who gets shrapnel in her leg at Bremen unfortunately has nothing to do with that," Mrs. Van Beusekom said. "War is truly horrible."

Nobody had an answer to that and the drone of aircraft faded. The carbide lamp dimmed slowly. Michiel went outside and stared through the dark toward the Knopper's house. Nothing could be seen or heard. Dirk is bound to be at home, he tried to reassure himself. He was just about to go back indoors when he heard a car coming. Instinctively he drew back against the wall. The car drove slowly on account of the blackout. It showed two small pinpoints of light. When it came to a stop right in front of Dirk's house, Michiel's heart missed a beat. A flashlight shone out and he pressed himself farther back against the wall. Two men walked up the front path and rang the bell loudly. They also kicked against the door with their heavy boots.

"*Mach auf!* Open up!"

Clearly the command was obeyed, because he heard Dirk's father's voice and more shouting in German that he could not understand. The soldiers went in and there was silence.

"It's all gone wrong," Michiel thought. "Dirk has

been caught, or else they have found out he took part in the raid." His heart was in his mouth. The back door opened and Mr. Van Beusekom called out in a soft voice, "Michiel, are you still in the barn?"

"I'm here," whispered Michiel, who was no more than a yard from his father. His father jumped, making a curious noise in his throat.

"Ssst."

"What are you doing, for God's sake?"

"They're searching Knopper's house."

Michiel's father listened. The only sound was a dog barking in the distance.

"How do you know?"

"I saw them go in. They kicked the door."

"I can't imagine Knopper doing anything against the Germans. What's more, they have German officers in the house. Are they searching all the houses?"

"No, they went to Knopper, no one else."

The Mayor remained thoughtful.

"Is this because of Dirk? He has a paper saying he is indispensable for his work. He need not work in Germany. Perhaps he is in the resistance."

Michiel clenched his teeth to stop himself from telling his father about the distribution office in Lowsand and the hidden letter. But he kept silent. Suddenly the neighbor's door opened. The men came out and walked to their car. As far as Michiel or his father could see, they had no one with them. Mrs. Knopper was standing in the doorway crying, "Don't shoot him, he is my only child. Don't shoot him!"

The car doors slammed and they drove off.

"I'll go and see them. Go and tell your mother," the Mayor said.

"All right."

Michiel went in. The visitors had gone to bed, but his mother was still busying herself in the kitchen by the light of a candle. He told her what they had seen.

"I'll wait until Father gets back," he said.

"Yes, all right, but get ready for bed."

Feeling his way, Michiel went upstairs. As he mounted the stairs to the attic, he was surprised by a faint light in his room.

"Don't be frightened," a voice said. "It's me." It was Uncle Ben.

"What are you doing here?"

"I was looking for an English dictionary," Uncle Ben whispered, "and I found one on your bookshelf. I have to write a note to a relative of mine in England, but my English is rather shaky. Ah, here it is: 'dynamite.' How stupid of me. Well, thank you. Good night."

"You can take the dictionary with you. I don't need it, now that I don't go to school. Most days I have more need of a German dictionary, I'm afraid."

"Oh no, it's not necessary. Thank you, anyway."

Uncle Ben disappeared in the little front room on the first floor where he usually slept. Michiel put on his pajamas and went down to the kitchen to keep his mother company. His father soon returned, looking upset.

"Dirk is said to have taken part in a raid on the distribution office at Lowsand. They caught him. One of the others appears to have been shot. The house next door was searched, but not very thoroughly, I would have said. Knopper and his wife are quite overcome."

"I can understand that," Mrs. Van Beusekom said. "Whatever will happen to Dirk now?"

Chapter 3

All night long Michiel's dreams were troubled by the letter. Whenever he woke up, he could think of nothing else. It seemed to him that this piece of paper could save Dirk's life. Who would want to be in his shoes? To be a prisoner of the Germans was dreadful, especially if they thought you know something and were determined to get it out of you. Tomorrow morning I must behave as normally as possible, Michiel thought. Nobody must suspect what I am doing. No one must know I'm going to Bertus Van Gelder. I have to be really careful. He felt as though he had not slept at all, yet suddenly it was morning.

He made his usual rounds and it was not until ten that he unobtrusively lifted the letter out of the hen house. He had to chase away a laying hen, which made a lot of fuss, but who would get suspicious of a clucking chicken? He hid the letter under his sweater and cycled off. He had quite a long way to go, since Bertus lived about six miles out of town.

That day, however, he was not to reach Bertus—his luck was completely out. First of all his extra-large tire came off. It was broken and he could not mend it himself. One bicycle repairer was not at home and a second did not have a new tire, so he had to repair the old one. The man took an hour and a half to finish the job.

At last Michiel was off again. But he was soon overtaken by a car. He knew exactly what that could mean and, sure enough, as if the pilot had sniffed them out, a fighter dived down. Michiel had quick reflexes. He leaped off his bicycle and jumped into the nearest manhole. These holes were dug along the roadside and were just big enough for one man. They could be found along every road and were dug for this very purpose. The car stopped and two German soldiers also ran for their lives, in the direction of a few tall trees. They were just in time. The fighter dived a second time, guns chattering. Michiel made himself as small as possible. His heart jumped when the bullets rattled on the road right by him.

The fighter flew off. The sound faded, and Michiel peered over the edge of the hole. The car was blazing. The two soldiers were not hurt, but one of the cows in the meadow nearby had been hit. The poor animal could not stand up and lowed pitifully. The two soldiers emerged from the trees and looked casually at their car. They shrugged their shoulders and walked off in the direction of the village.

Michiel felt the letter under his sweater. It was a great weight he wanted to get rid of, but the cow was moaning. He thought the land belonged to farmer Van Puttenstein, so he set off for the farmhouse. When he arrived, none of the men was at home. Mrs. Van Puttenstein could not walk very well because of rheumatism and in the end Michiel had to go for the butcher himself. He was furious and almost beside himself with frustration. Not until three o'clock could he set off for the third time to see Bertus. He was nearly halfway there when someone caught up with him. When he saw who it was, Michiel's heart leaped with fear. Mr. Schafter!

"Well now, isn't it the Mayor's son?"

"Good afternoon, Mr. Schafter."

"Where are you off to in such a hurry? Is there a fire?"

Everyone knew that Schafter was not to be trusted. He was always hanging around the German barracks and sat with the Germans in their mess. He also did odd jobs for them and he was suspected of betraying a Jewish family who were caught hiding with the Van Hunnens. They were sent to Germany and so were the Van Hunnens. Nobody had heard from them since. That was why Michiel answered quickly, "I have to go to Lowsand to Alderman Van Kleiweg."

"Well, that's nice. I'm going there too. Let's cycle together." Under his breath Michiel uttered every swear word he knew, but there was nothing he could do. He simply had to go to Lowsand instead of to Bertus. What he was going to say to the Alderman when he got there he could not think. He did not know if the Alderman was pro- or anti-German. While Schafter was chatting away about this, that and the other thing, Michiel racked his brains for an excuse to turn around and go back. But his mind was a blank.

"Did you hear about the raid on the distribution office?" Schafter asked.

"They were talking about it this morning," Michiel said, immediately suspicious.

"Who were talking?"

"How should I know? Just some people."

"Have you a message for Van Kleiweg from your father?"

"Actually, I'm taking him a blanket for the baby," Michiel answered.

"Oh well, I just thought," Schafter said cheerfully, as if he hadn't noticed Michiel's annoyance at all.

A quarter of an hour later they reached the Alderman's house. He answered the door saying cheerfully, "Do come in."

"I can't wait, I'm afraid. I simply have a message from my father that the waterworks committee meeting will be next Tuesday at the usual time."

"Oh, thanks. Four o'clock on Tuesday. Tell your father I'll be there. Good-bye!"

"Good day, gentlemen," said Michiel.

"I will only be five minutes and then we could go back together," said Schafter. "Can't you just wait?"

But Michiel could not stand Schafter's company and his constant probing.

"I'm in a hurry. I'm sorry. Next time, perhaps?" he said, and off he went, pedaling as fast as he could, to Vlank. The letter crackled under his sweater, but he did not dare go directly to Bertus. First of all he had to make sure about that meeting. He had heard his father discussing it. He wondered if he should tell his father about the letter. He decided against it. "As long as I can keep this to myself, I will, even if it does mean a few more miles on my bike."

Fortunately his father was at home.

"Father, I'm going to Lowsand. Didn't I hear you say something about a meeting of the waterworks committee? Shall I give a message to Van Kleiweg?" He told the lie without blinking an eyelid.

"Good thing you reminded me. I wanted the meeting Wednesday, usual time."

"Wednesday at four?"

"Yes. Thanks a lot."

"'Bye."

"Where are you going?"

Michiel muttered something about buying a hen for "that woman from Amsterdam who is staying at that farmhouse, you know," and slipped out of the room. That was all right. Father wouldn't ask any more. What a bore, to have to go to Lowsand again. He had hoped he had picked the right day, because those meetings often were on Tuesdays. Oh well, better get it over with. Naturally, he met Schafter on the way. He looked puzzled, but Michiel waved his hand and laughed at the idea of the man wondering why he was rushing up and down to Lowsand. Well, he didn't have second sight; but, then, he wasn't shortsighted either. He told the alderman he had made a mistake about the day, and just had time to reach home before dark. Bertus would have to wait until tomorrow. To be quite safe, he put the letter back in the henhouse, hoping there had been nothing in it that had needed doing that very day. He was very unhappy. Dirk was in prison and he had not even managed to carry out that one simple task. Moreover, he was tired from all the cycling. All sorts of unknown people came in as usual. Uncle Ben had left. Erica took the flashlight for half an hour, just to comb her hair. Jochem sniffed every two minutes. It had been a rotten day altogether.

Chapter 4

The next day was even worse. As early as he could possibly slip away, Michiel was on his bicycle. He reached Bertus's farmhouse without difficulty. There was no one to be seen in the farmyard, but the dog barked as if its tail were on fire. Michiel went into the house—it was empty. Where *were* Bertus and his wife Jannechin? Everything was open, so somebody should have been at home.

"Hello," he called. Just then he heard the clanking of pails. In the ramshackle barn he found Jannechin struggling to carry two heavy buckets. She was feeding the pigs.

"Hey, Jannechin!"

"The Mayor's Michiel! Any news of Bertus?"

"News of Bertus?"

The little woman's face fell and she put down the pails.

"I thought the Mayor would perhaps know what they've done to my Bertus."

"Done to Bertus?"

"Didn't you even know that they came and took Bertus away yesterday?"

"Who, the Boche?"

"Yes, of course, who else?"

"What had he done?"

Jannechin stamped her foot angrily. "He didn't do anything. He was feeding the pigs, just as I am now. They examined everything, even his clothes, but they found nothing. Absolutely nothing."

"And they took him all the same?"

"Yes, the scoundrels. I let the dog loose and it jumped and got one of 'em by the throat. But the others beat the animal off with their guns. It's a wonder they didn't shoot him."

Michiel felt miserable.

"When did this happen?"

"About half past four."

Michiel reflected. It was just coincidence. Schafter could not have guessed anything. What time was it when he met him for the second time? About four. So that he couldn't have had anything to do with it.

"Listen, Jannechin, did they visit other farm-houses," he asked, "or just yours?"

"Only us, I think. They come straight here with their damn cars and you know, Mick, if Bertus had done anything—and God knows that I knew none of it, if he had—then he was betrayed."

"How do you know?" Michiel was startled.

"Yesterday evening when he had gone, I was that upset that I went to see my sister. You know, the one—she married Hendrik den Otter. They live right on the corner of Dirmans Lane."

"Yes, I know them."

"Now then, I go in their house and tell them that they have taken Bertus. My sister says, 'Oh, no, love. Was that about half past fourish? Saw two cars going your way. If I'd known they were coming for you, I'd have done something to hold them up.' 'What would you have done?' I ask her. 'Well, something,' says she."

"You were talking about treason, Jannechin. What has that to do with treason?"

"Oh, yes my sister said the Boche talked to someone in the street, and when they'd stopped talking they went your way. And that man pointed them the way."

"Who was the man?"

"Oh, what's his name? He's that whey-faced fellow, and he's always cycling around."

"You mean Schafter?"

"Yes, that's the one, Schafter. They say he's no good."

Michiel was silent. Somehow he felt guilty, but how could Schafter have guessed anything? Even if he had suspected that Michiel's visit to Van Kleiweg wasn't genuine he still couldn't have guessed that Bertus was involved. He must get away from here to sort out his thoughts.

"I must go, Jannechin. I do hope Bertus comes back soon."

"Tell your father. Can he do anything?"

"I'll certainly tell him, but I doubt if he can do anything. 'Bye, and all the best to you."

Fortunately, she had not asked why he had come. He cycled away quickly.

After a while he got off his bike and sat down with his back to a large tree to think things over. What was the sequence of events? First, Dirk had told him about the raid and then handed him the letter for Bertus. He himself had put the letter away. Nobody could have seen that. Then the raid had failed. One man was shot trying to get away, and Dirk had been taken away. He, Michiel, tried to take the letter to Bertus the next morning, but had failed. Stupid! He could have walked when his tire broke. Perhaps Schafter noticed that he was lying to the Alderman and he saw him for the second time about four o'clock, going to Lowsand. At half past four he showed the Boche the way to Bertus's place when they asked him. It just did not make sense. Schafter *couldn't* have known.

Suddenly he realized what must have happened. Dirk had talked. They must have tortured him so much that he had mentioned Bertus's name, and Schafter's part was only to show them the way. He shivered when he thought of what they must have done to Dirk to make him talk. Dirk was not the type to give up without a fight. Suddenly, a second, more frightening, thought struck him. Had Dirk also mentioned that Michiel had a letter for Bertus? That must have been what the Boche were searching for—the letter! They expected it to have been delivered by half past four. But that meant that they might be waiting for him at home. Then they would catch him and find the letter. That must not happen.

Michiel took out the envelope. He wanted to destroy it, tear it into a thousand pieces and bury it under the sand. Should he read it first? No, better not. Then, if he was caught, he could not possibly disclose what was in it. He must get rid of it. He ripped the letter in two and then tore it apart again.

Then he hesitated. What if it was something very important? Of course it must be, otherwise Dirk would not have written it. Bertus could do nothing about the matter now, so he must do it. Of this, he was suddenly certain. It was a haunting thought.

For a good five minutes he sat motionless, staring at the pieces in his hands. If he read the letter, he would become a part of the resistance. But if he did not read it . . . no, that was all wrong. He had no choice. He had already joined the resistance when he agreed to take the letter. He took the four pieces, pieced them together and began to read:

When you read this, I shall have been caught by the Germans. Do you remember the air battle over Vlank, three weeks ago, when an English pilot was shot down? The pilot parachuted to the ground, but the Germans could not find him. I was more successful. I found him. He was hurt: his leg and shoulder. I took him with me. The wound has been dressed and the leg is in plaster, done by an expert. Don't ask who. I then had the problem of hiding him. Do you remember I worked '41–42, in the forest reserve? We planted many trees in the Dagdaler woods. There I dug an underground hideout. There are four squares of young trees, each about 3 acres. The hideout is in the middle of the northeast square. The entrance is in a thicket of young fir trees. Nobody could possibly find it. That's where the pilot is hidden. I took food to him every second day. He cannot walk, so if you don't take something to him, he will starve. Be careful: he is very suspicious and has a gun. It is difficult to talk to him, as he only speaks English, and I am afraid your English is no better than mine. Nobody knows about this hideout, so take care not to give it away.

Michiel read the letter three times. Then he tore it up into tiny pieces and buried them. He suddenly felt very calm, in spite of the tight knot in the pit of his stomach. He was going to harbor an English pilot, a crime punishable by death. The only question was, how much had Dirk said? As little as possible, he was sure. Perhaps he had only mentioned Bertus's name and kept Michiel's secret. He would have to sneak home and find out if the Germans had been looking for him. But it was too early for that. He must first go to the pilot. He might not have eaten for two days. Where could he get food for him? At home? That would be unwise. Van de Werf lived nearby and Michiel was popular there, so he got on his bike.

Mrs. Van de Werf was busy cleaning the baking house.

"'Morning, Michiel," said Mrs. Van de Werf.

"Good morning, Mrs. Van de Werf. Fine weather today."

"You're right about that. My word, you've grown!

Take care the Boche don't take you off to work in
Germany. How old are you?"

"Nearly sixteen."

"Well, they took my brother's son in Oosterwolde
last week. He was working in a factory. True, he was
seventeen, but . . . you know, they take them younger every day."

"I'll lie low."

"What did you want? Something to eat?"

"Well, if possible."

"And what would you like?"

"A piece of ham, if that's not asking too much?"

"Well, as it's you . . . "

They went into the house together. Hanging in the
chimney were two big hams, and bacon and sausages.
Mrs. Van de Werf took a ham off the hook and sliced
off a fair-sized piece.

"Here you are."

"Thanks ever so much, Mrs. Van de Werf." Michiel
paid and started to go.

"Wouldn't you like a nice piece of my bread-and-
cheese?"

"Oh, yes, please!"

The woman cut a slice off a big round loaf which
she held against her chest, put butter and cheese on it
and handed it to Michiel. It was a meal in itself.
Anyone from a big city would have been glad to pay a
pound for it.

"Thanks, I'll eat it on my way home," Michiel said.
"I must run now."

"Off you go, then, boy."

Once out of sight, Michiel opened the wrapping

around the ham and put the bread-and-cheese in it as
well. Then he went off toward Dagdaler woods.

He found the northeast square without difficulty.
Making quite sure that no one had seen him, he hid
his bicycle some way off, for he had to go under the
bushes. He made his way on foot for the last half-
mile. The wood was silent, the autumn sun shone
through the trees, and the silence was broken only by
birds singing.

Michiel looked carefully around as he approached
the young plantation. The young trees were so closely
packed together that he could see no way through
them. How on earth was he to get to the hideout?
Then he noticed that, close to the ground, there were
fewer branches. He could crawl. It was hard work and
his face and arms were scratched by the prickly
branches. Ever so often, he stood upright to see where
he was and to check that he was still alone. At last, he
was near the middle, but where was the hideout? He
struggled on trying not to make a noise, though he
could not help snapping some small twigs.

"Don't move!"

Startled, Michiel froze. The strange voice was very
close. Lowering his own voice, he said, "Friend."
Why he said that he didn't know. Perhaps he had read
it somewhere. No, it was what Jannechin said to her
dog!

"Who are you?"

Michiel knew what that meant, from his English
lessons at school.

"Dirk's friend," he said.

"Where is Dirk?"

"In prison."

"Come closer," the Englishman demanded, and Michiel obeyed by crawling closer to the voice. Now he could see narrow steps going down. A young man, about twenty years old, was standing at the side of the entrance. Part of the trouser legs of his uniform had been cut off to accommodate the plaster. His right arm was in a sling and his jacket was draped over his shoulders. He had a thick beard. In his left hand he held a gun. He gestured to Michiel to come down.

It was very dark inside, but once Michiel's eyes were accustomed to it, he saw how the hideout was constructed. A broad, deep hole had been made and small tree trunks supported the sides. A large wooden door, or something of the sort, formed the ceiling or roof. This was covered with earth. The little trees planted on this were scraggly. Perhaps there was too little earth for them. The hideout was about ten feet long and six feet wide. Dirk had made a good job of it, but to stay in it day and night with a broken leg! In one corner was a heap of dry leaves and two plain blankets. Michiel also saw a bottle, a cup, and an old woolen shawl. That was all. Good heavens, to think this man had been here for weeks!

They started to talk with difficulty. The pilot realized that he had to speak very slowly and Michiel searched his memory to find the words he had learned at school. And they managed to communicate. The pilot was called Jack and was happy to have somebody to talk to, because with Dirk, who had never done languages at school, conversation had been even more limited. When he heard that Dirk had been caught and might have started talking, he became very nervous. The Englishman was anxious about Dirk and for himself. Had Dirk revealed the hideout?

In spite of his fears, he ate the ham with pleasure. He had nothing to drink and Michiel realized that he should have thought of bringing water. Jack asked him if he could return tomorrow with drink and more food.

"O.K.," said Michiel, feeling very proud that he knew a real expression in such a difficult language. He also thought, providing I'm not caught like Dirk. But he said nothing of the sort, not only because he did not know the English words.

The pilot showed him the path, or rather the little stairway, Dirk had used to get in and out, and he was soon out of the fir thicket. Always being careful of snakes, Michiel looked carefully around before removing his bike from the bushes. As he emerged from the wood, he double-checked to make sure that nobody had spotted him. Before going home, he went first to Dirk's parents. They were still very upset, but he had no difficulty directing the conversation around to the search of the house—the poor people could talk of nothing else.

"Did the Germans search any other houses today?" he asked.

"Not that I know of," Mr. Knopper said.

"I'm always scared they'll take my father," Michiel said.

"Now that they've taken our Dirk we can understand your fear . . . " and Mr. Knopper started all over again, talking about his own misery.

Michiel was now almost convinced that the Germans had not been searching for him. His neighbors would certainly have known. Nevertheless, he was rather nervous as he entered the house through the back door after putting his bike in the barn. But his mother said cheerfully, "There you are, then, Michiel. What did you do with yourself today?"

So it was all right.

"Nothing special. I went here, there and everywhere."

His mother took no notice. The evening passed. He felt an irresistible urge to take someone into his confidence—his father, his mother—but he was able to suppress it. "A good resistance worker works on his own," he had once heard his father say. "He is alone with his task and with what he knows."

Michiel was well aware that his task was an adult one, and that from now on it was a question of life and death. Well, he had always hated being treated like a child and now he had his chance to behave like a man, so he said nothing. He expected his mother to read from his face that he had something on his mind and perhaps she would say, "A penny for your thoughts." He kept thinking he heard the police coming. He also wondered how he would manage to get enough food for Jack during the next few weeks. But he said nothing.

Chapter 5

It was not easy for Michiel to visit the pilot every other day. He lied continually to get extra food; and he had to invent new reasons to explain his frequent absences.

Being the Mayor's son, it was fairly easy for Michiel to buy food from farmhouses in the area. He did not worry that his hard-earned savings were slowly vanishing. It was for a good cause. Besides, everybody said that, after the war, money would not be worth anything anyway.

The main problem was preventing his parents from finding out that, although he bought food in such quantities, so little of it appeared at home. So, once in a while, he brought some food home. He took the further precaution of buying from farmhouses that were farther away from the village.

All in all, it was a man's job. But Michiel did not mind. He was grateful that the Boche had not come for him. Dirk clearly had not mentioned his name. Perhaps he had mentioned Bertus because he knew nothing and because they would not find anything in his house. After a while they would probably release him. Dirk must have counted on Michiel to keep the pilot alive. But that did not seem quite logical, because Dirk had obviously reckoned on Michiel taking the letter straight to Bertus. Maybe Dirk had given in quickly, to be sure they would arrest Bertus before he got the letter from Michiel. In his heart of hearts Michiel considered that Dirk had talked rather too soon, but he suppressed the thought. What would he do himself if they broke his jaw or something even worse?

In the meantime, Jack was not so easy to manage. He became bored, and he was anxious about his shoulder wound, which seemed to be healing too slowly. The circumstances were hardly favorable: a cold, damp hole, with a heap of leaves for a bed, was not the ideal convalescent home. Michiel did what he could. He stole English books from his father's bookcase. Jack was particularly entranced by a book about natural healing from the last century. It had beautiful pictures of swinging baths, steam baths, and showers, and even a closed envelope for students older than eighteen. There was also a book about pumping stations, a detective story by Agatha Christie—a real godsend—a handbook on the combustion engine, and a few other volumes. He was so glad to have these books in his own language and read them so often that he practically learned them by heart.

Michiel tried to make life a little more comfortable for his guest. He could not take a bed to the woods, but he acquired some more blankets and even managed to get a small folding chair for Jack. He also took some wood, nails, and a hammer to the hideout. One day when the woodcutters were working, so that a little noise would not be noticed, he hammered together a door to close off the cold entrance to the underground chamber. Because of his injured shoulder, Jack could not do the job himself. This was a pity, because the pilot was becoming more and more depressed and activity would have helped. Michiel had only once managed to get a bandage, which was now dirty, and the wound, far from improving, was obviously getting worse. He realized he must get some kind of help.

But who? He didn't know if he could trust any of the doctors he knew. The district nurse? He did not know her very well. Any other nurse? Of course, why had he not thought of that before! His sister, Erica, had been training to be a nurse in Zwolle, the town where he went to school. Like him, she could not go there either, but she might know something about these things. But could he trust Erica? Of course he could. He was becoming so distrustful he would soon begin to suspect his own mother of being a German spy. Would Erica be prepared to do it? Would Jack like the idea? Would it be wise to tell Erica where the hideout was? Could he perhaps get Jack somewhere else for a short time?

Michiel suddenly wondered how Jack with a hurt shoulder and a broken leg had managed to reach the hideout in the first place. He asked the pilot.

"Don't ask me," Jack replied with a wry expression on his face. He explained that Dirk had put him on his side and pulled him, by his healthy leg, through the thicket. He would rather be tortured by the Germans than have to go through that hell again. That, of course, was just a joke, but certainly it could not have been a pleasant trip!

"The war will soon be over," said Michiel. "It has already lasted exactly four and a half years and one day, for Holland at least."

"And how many minutes?" asked Jack. He was studying Dutch and improving all the time. Michiel had dug up a little book of which he found an English as well as a Dutch edition, and he had given both to Jack. So he had given up studying about natural ways of healing and all the different kinds of health baths.

"We must find somebody to look after your wound," Michiel said.

"Impossible."

"It's got to be done."

Jack shrugged his shoulders. Doing so gave him so much pain that he swore, and not in Dutch!

"You know yourself we must do something," said Michiel. Jack looked at the dirty dressing.

"And just what do you propose to do? Get someone from the German military hospital?"

"My sister," said Michiel.

"Your sister?" Jack said, not sure if he had heard correctly.

"Yes, my sister. She is a trained nurse." He did not mention that her experience was very limited.

"Can you trust her?"

Michiel looked hurt. "You could trust our white mice," he said.

"I mean, can she take responsibility?"

Michiel had to think that over. Could Erica take responsibility? She did nothing but giggle with her friends, and during such spells, Michiel wished her at the other end of the world. Then again, she was forever combing her hair in front of the mirror. On the other hand, it was true that she often helped their mother. And last night she had announced that she was going into some kind of assistance work, whatever that might mean. But taking responsibility? No, she could never do that.

"Okay," said Jack, "let's forget the idea."

"Wait a minute," suggested Michiel. "If you weren't wearing your uniform, but some ordinary overcoat, which I could bring here, and if you were to hold your tongue, she might not know you were British. Then I would blindfold her before coming here and again when we left. That way it would be safe enough to take the chance."

"Hey," Jack said, "does your sister do what you tell her to? English sisters wouldn't do what their brothers say."

"Sometimes they do, one can never be sure," said Michiel, smiling.

———————

Whether from a sense of adventure, or simply out of curiosity, Erica agreed. The bandage made it very exciting.

"Don't you think I'll look a bit queer crossing the street blindfolded?"

"I'll put the bandage on when we are out of sight of everybody."

"Well, couldn't I shut my eyes and then we could walk arm in arm, as if we were a couple in love?"

"How could I be in love with my sister?" Michiel demanded.

"Who's the injured person?"

"You must not know. The less you know, the less dangerous it will be. You must promise me not to speak to the stranger. . . ." Michiel's voice was very serious.

"Oh, aren't we grown-up?" Erica mocked.

"You promise that?"

"Yes, and I will also keep my eyes shut when I go through the wood. I swear." She put two fingers in the air. Michiel was not impressed, she was always swearing to do something, but he had to take the chance.

"Have you got your dressings and stuff?"

Erica nodded.

"How did you get them?"

"I have my secret sources."

"O.K., you needn't tell me your secrets, I don't tell you mine."

The next morning Michiel took to the hideout an old dirty jacket on which a hen had hatched her eggs. In the afternoon he and Erica went together. Michiel took all the precautions that had become a habit. They cycled by a roundabout way and he remembered to look around carefully before they entered the woods to make sure that nobody spotted them. Erica thought it all nonsense, but Michiel had always been more careful than his sister and for once she had to leave it all to him. He took no notice of her protests.

Once in the wood, they hid their bicycles under the bushes and continued on foot. Feeling a little self-conscious, Michiel walked arm in arm with his sister.

Occasionally Michiel glanced at her to see if she was keeping her eyes shut. She was really very good about it. After a while Michiel whispered, "Now on your knees. You can open your eyes, if you promise to look only at me, not to look around. I'll go first."

When Jack saw Erica, he exclaimed, "Boy!"

Michiel kicked his good leg to warn him, and Jack kept quiet. Erica started to undo the dressing in a very efficient way. The week before, when Michiel had done the same thing, Jack had moaned several times. Now he was silent.

Just shows how good Erica is at such things, Michiel thought, proud of his sister. He did not realize that a man does not show pain in the presence of a lovely girl, and to consider Erica beautiful had never entered his mind.

In the meantime Erica cleaned the edges of the wound with a piece of cotton-wool. Then she sprinkled a disinfectant powder on the open part and covered it with a piece of sterilized cloth. After that she bandaged the whole dressing, and Jack looked much better than he had half an hour earlier. He was happy and had difficulty in not speaking.

"How long has that leg been in plaster?" Erica asked.

"Five weeks," Michiel replied. "It should have another three, though."

Erica nodded her agreement.

"I'll take it off," she said. "And that dressing should be changed once a week, so I'll come back in seven days."

Jack nodded enthusiastically.

"Well, let's get going," Michiel said, a little annoyed. He did not like all this talking and he was not pleased with the proposed schedule of visits. He would have to have a word with Erica later.

They left and reached home without incident.

"Don't think you're going to visit him every week," Michiel said.

"What do you mean?" Erica asked in her vaguest manner.

"You're not to go there again."

"Why not? I did my best, didn't I?"

"Yes, but it's too dangerous for two of us. It's bad enough that I have to go so often."

"All right, you are in charge."

Michiel looked at her questioningly. She did not seem to be joking, but instead was quite serious. Well, it's useful having a sister, sometimes, Michiel thought.

It turned out that the dressing of his wound was not only good for Jack's body but also for his state of mind. When Michiel visited him two days later he was very cheerful and said that he felt worlds better. There was only one thing that troubled him: his mother. His mother lived in Nottingham and he was her only son. Two daughters had died before he had been born, and she was always overanxious about him. He had joined the Air Force to get away from all that fussing around—but also for another reason.

"What was that?" Michiel asked.

Jack had been trying to speak Dutch, but now he used English to explain: "My father was killed at Dunkirk in 1940. He went across the Channel with a small boat to pick up soldiers trying to get back to England. It was the time when the Jerries swept through France at a terrific rate and so many thousands in the British Army were caught in a trap."

Michiel nodded.

"The boat was bombed," Jack said. "Direct hit. It was bad enough for me, but my mother—well, she was absolutely lost."

"And now your mother will be anxious about you."

"Anxious? She won't be getting much sleep, she'll have lost so much weight and got so many gray hairs that she must be the sorriest-looking sight in all

England. They presumably told her I was lost, which usually means that you are dead, but sometimes a note gets through from a P.O.W. camp."

"So you think your mother will be sitting on the doorstep of the post office every morning?"

"Well, these notes normally come via the Red Cross, so she may be sitting there. But, you know, I do wish I could relieve her mind. Couldn't you possibly smuggle a note for me?"

Michiel sighed. It was not easy taking care of a pilot all by yourself.

"Well, I'll think about it," he said. "How did you like my sister?"

Jack's tongue clicked his approval.

"Tops," he said. "And my shoulder is ever so much better. What a shame I could not talk to her."

"Such is life in an occupied country," said Michiel philosophically. "What else might the King's servant require?"

"Nothing. This is the best hotel I know of. Only my mother, if you . . ."

"I'll think about it." Michiel repeated. He crawled out on all fours and set off for the village.

———

Blast! Michiel thought. How am I going to get a letter to England? Of course, there was no normal postal service with enemy countries of Germany. He could try to contact the resistance—he had a hunch that Dries Grotenhuis had something to do with it—but he did not want to give himself away. "A good resistance worker works on his own; alone with his task and with what he knows," he kept repeating to himself. Nevertheless, the idea of Jack's mother sitting on the doorstep of the Red Cross office kept him busy. What *could* he do? There was one way he could get a message to England, but was it wise? In fact he had thought of it immediately when Jack asked him: Uncle Ben. He knew escape routes and could surely get a small note to England. But still . . . it meant taking a third person into his confidence. However, Jack kept insisting, until eventually Michiel gave in.

"Okay, write your note," he said. "But nothing in it that can give your position away."

"Right," Jack said, and wrote that he was alive and not in German hands; that he was slightly wounded, but nothing serious. His mother need not worry, because he was well looked after by a fine young man of sixteen. This was flattering for Michiel, but it was unnecessary, so the sentence had to be dropped. Like it or not, Jack had to write the letter again.

Two days later, Uncle Ben arrived. Michiel invited him for a walk and said, "You told me about ways of escape for British soldiers. Could you get a letter to England for me?"

Uncle Ben gave Michiel a keen glance. "What kind of letter?"

"A paper one."

Uncle Ben chuckled, but not for long. His face grew earnest. He took Michiel's arm, saying, "Don't tell me you are involved in the resistance?"

"Oh, no! A friend of my friend's brother wants to send it. Can you do it for me?"

"Who is this friend with the brother?"

"So you can't do it," Michiel said, not wishing to be interrogated. "It's getting rather cold, isn't it?"

"Good for you," Uncle Ben said. "You're the right type. Give me the letter."

Michiel took it from his pocket.

"Here you are."

"Thanks."

After that, the letter wasn't mentioned again.

"The letter is on its way," Michiel told Jack, and then suddenly he accused him: "Your wound has been dressed."

Jack nodded kindly.

"Erica?"

"Yes."

"The little brat! How did she know where to find you?"

"Don't know," said Jack. "Perhaps she didn't shut her eyes too tightly the other day. She thought the bandage needed changing and was afraid you wouldn't let her do it. That is why she . . . she . . ."

"So you talked to her?" Michiel asked. Jack looked guilty.

"Does she know you are a pilot?"

"I'm afraid she guessed. She's not stupid, you know. My Dutch is fairly good, but, you know, some words give me away. . . ."

"Man, don't be silly. Every second word you say is as English as Queen Victoria. Well, you can expect to be caught any moment now. I can't keep you safe this way. And you, me, Erica, and my father will all be shot. Bang, bang, bang."

"Erica won't talk."

"No, she won't talk, but she isn't cautious enough. She doesn't make sure that nobody sees her. She leaves traces. When a man like Schafter sees her going to the wood he'll get suspicious."

"Who is Schafter?"

"Oh, never mind, just a fellow I know who's a Nazi. I'm off to give Erica a telling-off. Perhaps we'll be lucky and get away with it."

"Did you say you'd sent the letter?"

"It's safely on its way. 'Bye."

"Cheerio."

———

Michiel scolded Erica as well as he could, but it was not easy trying to scold someone in a whisper, and his mother was in the next room. It was almost as bad as being mad at someone, leaving the room, slamming the door, and then having to go back to fetch your gloves—you felt like such a fool. Michiel had no influence on his sister at all. True, she looked guilty and said she would not do it again, but she did not sound as though she meant it. And once Michiel had stopped, she said she thought that the wound was a great deal better and that she was so pleased! What could Michiel say after that? He impressed on her that she must not tell anybody, not even their father, and that was as much as he could do. A week went by without any thing special happening, meaning nothing out of the ordinary, everyday events.

And then Uncle Ben appeared again. This time it

was his turn to take Michiel for a walk and he asked, "Do you ever meet that friend of yours? The one who has a brother who also has a friend?"

Michiel was on his guard straight away.

"No," he said stiffly.

"What a shame. I have a letter from his mother. Now what am I to do with it? Well, I'll put it under this loose strip of bark. Then I am rid of it." He went up to a tree and lodged it behind the loose bark. Then he turned around and went home without looking back.

Rather surprised, Michiel went up to the tree and removed the envelope. Nothing was written on it. Could it be for Jack? Of course it could. Perhaps Uncle Ben had given his own address in order to get an answer. Anyway, he would take it to Jack.

With even more than his usual caution he went to the hideout. Could there be anything in the envelope to help someone to follow him and find out where Jack was? Was Uncle Ben following him now? Of course not. He really must stop being so suspicious. Uncle Ben was all right. And so it turned out. When Jack had opened the envelope he grinned. It was a letter from his overjoyed mother. She had imagined him dead a dozen times. She had even enclosed a snapshot of herself in the garden. How could Uncle Ben have managed that in such a short time?

Chapter 6

It is a November morning in 1944. All is quiet in
the village. The clouds hang low, so there are no
planes. Only a few cars are still left. It has been
raining all night. The rain has stopped, but the
trees are still dripping. The streets glisten. A black
cat runs across the street and disappears into a
barn.

The village is gripped with fear. No one dares
venture outside, if they can avoid it. A woman in
clogs removes some wet clothes from the washing
line and scurries inside. A rumor has reached the
village, but nobody knows from where. The news
has simply crept in. Yesterday, or perhaps the
night before, a couple of German soldiers had

found the body of a colleague. At first he was thought to have been a deserter. But now they know he had been murdered about six weeks ago.

What will happen now? How will the Germans take revenge? Some horrible cases of retribution have been heard of, following an attack on a soldier. How true are these stories? How can one defend oneself? Basically, one cannot. Everybody simply keeps quiet. The low clouds seem to reflect the menace hanging over the village. Below, fear walks in the streets, in the gardens, and in the houses. The village waits motionless for the future to reveal itself.

––––––––

At ten o'clock in the morning an armored car speeds through Vlank. Now they dare to come, now that the clouds are low and no Spitfire can see them. Brakes screeching, the car pulls up in front of the town hall. Eight soldiers jump out. They kick open the door with their heavy boots and enter. It does not take long. They emerge with the Mayor and the secretary, whose heads are held high as they walk between the soldiers.

There was just a fleeting glimpse of them before the car doors closed. The car sped on: to the vet, the notary, the priest, the headmaster, and the rich farmer Schilthuis. Ten people in all were taken to the barracks on the road to Zwolle. The captives were not allowed to take anything with them. They were given no indication of what to expect. Their wives, who wanted to protect them, were rudely pushed aside. How long did it all last? No more than an hour. When the car left, the peaceful village scene had changed. A nervous stream of talking, crying, guessing, consoling, hysterical, powerless, and encouraging people went in and out of each other's houses, knowing they were absolutely helpless.

———————

"Reprisal victim" is the term used when someone is punished for something done by someone else. Immediately after their imprisonment the German commanding officer announced that the ten people would be hanged from the trees in the marketplace if the culprit did not give himself up.

Erica vomited when she heard the news. Mrs. Van Beusekom had dark lines under her eyes. Her cheekbones seemed to stand out more than usual and a nervous twitch played around her mouth. She gave Jochem a clean, white piece of paper and a pencil, to amuse himself with some drawing. He was too young to understand. Then she went and stood next to Michiel, who sat in a chair, staring out of the window.

"I'll go and see them," she said.

"Where to? The barracks?"

"The commander. I met him twice. He seemed like a reasonable fellow to me. I'll plead with him not to carry out his threat."

"Shall I do it?" Michiel asked.

"No. I think I had better go."

Michiel realized she was right. As the wife of the

Mayor, she naturally had more chance of making an impression. After all, he was not quite sixteen, and a mere boy.

Mrs. Van Beusekom changed into a dark blue suit. She powdered over the dark lines under her eyes and went to the barracks. Michiel watched her go. How he admired her. What could he do? He must think it out quietly. Who could possibly have killed the soldier? How could one find out? It might be someone from another village, or poachers who were spotted and did it in self-defense. Or the boys in the resistance movement. That was unlikely. They were not as foolish as all that. Everybody knew that killing a German meant fearful reprisals from the *Wehrmacht.* However, it was possible that the resistance had some information about it. But he did not know who was in it, except for Dirk and Bertus, and they'd been captured.

Who else might be in it? Michiel thought about the men in the village: Dries Grotenhuis was probably one of them, but he was not a careful man; Mr. Postma, the schoolteacher. Of course! Michiel remembered his history lessons in the fourth form, when Mr. Postma told them about the Eighty Years' War and the strong sense of freedom held by the Dutch people. Michiel's father had sometimes jokingly reminded him that not only Dutch people had a longing for freedom, but still . . . Mr. Postma was sure to be in the resistance.

Michiel put on his ragged old coat and went to see him. Stupidly, he had forgotten that Mr. Postma would be at school. He had to wait until twelve, but finally he met the schoolteacher in his front garden.

"Hello, sir."

"Hello, Michiel."

There was no gladness in these greetings. Each of them realized that the other was thinking about the Mayor, the headmaster, and the others.

"Do you know who killed that German?" Michiel asked. Mr. Postma shook his head.

"Then do you know who is the head of the resistance in Vlank?" Again Mr. Postma shook his head, though a trifle more slowly than the first time. Michiel looked him straight in the face.

"If you meet him by any chance, would you give him a message?" Postma was silent.

"Would you tell him that the man who did it must, simply must, surrender to the Germans?"

Almost imperceptibly, Mr. Postma nodded.

"All the best to you and your mother," he said. "And now I must be going," he continued with a faint smile, which, with a considerable stretch of the imagination, might just have been a smile of understanding.

"Good day, Michiel."

With no great hope that his mission would prove fruitful, Michiel went home, to find his mother resting on a chair in the kitchen. The commander had refused to see her.

Time dragged. The weather was oppressive. The

stream of passersby was thinner than on other days. Had they heard what was happening in the village, or was it the weather? Nevertheless, hundreds of people passed along the Zuiderzee street that day. One of them was an old man pulling a rickety cart. It was really a kind of beach carriage on wooden wheels, meant for wheeling two young babies along the sands. But instead of babies he was hauling a sack of potatoes. Just in front of the Mayor's house, one wheel split in two. The old man did not know what to do, he simply could not cope. He pulled, pushed, and heaved at the cart and in the end just sat down on a stone, staring helplessly into the distance. Michiel went up to him. It was a reflex action, but he was so used to helping these people that his legs automatically carried him.

"Wheel broken," he stated.

The old man nodded.

"Shall we get it mended?"

The man looked up in surprise. He had not thought of that.

"Is that possible?"

"Perhaps. Just wait a minute." Michiel went into the barn to fetch his tools. Then he took the wheel off the axle.

"If you stay here, I'll take it to the cartwright. Okay?"

The old man nodded. He did not seem very alert. Michiel jumped on his bicycle.

When he entered the workshop, the cartwright looked as if he had seen a ghost, but he was only too glad to stop his work and repair the wheel. He's so helpful, it's as if I had made a dying request, thought Michiel.

The wheel was repaired in half an hour and Michiel cycled back with it. As he passed the marketplace he suddenly noticed the seven strong chestnut trees. There were more than enough sturdy branches for hanging ten people. But that could not happen. It was impossible to think that they would put such a fine, intelligent, kind, handsome man as his father on a rope and . . . It must not happen. It must not!

But it could happen, Michiel knew. It had happened for less reason. In a French village they had hanged all the menfolk from the lampposts. And the other day one of the passersby had told them the story of a family in Gouda, or was it in Woerden? The Germans had found weapons in the house of a couple with six children. They took the whole family out into the garden and shot the father and his two eldest sons right before the eyes of the mother and the younger children. Such things were happening more often, now that the Boche knew they were losing the war.

Michiel swallowed. He felt sick. But summoning up all his willpower, he forced himself to ride past the trees. He found the old man still sitting on his little stone. He looked relieved when he saw the mended wheel.

"How is that possible?" he muttered.

"With a few clamps and an iron band."

"Unbelievable. How much do I owe you?"

"Three guilders."

"Here you are, and two quarters for yourself."
Michiel could not help smiling. Two quarters! To
think he would ever ask money for his odd jobs. How
much would he have to ask for looking after Jack? But
he thanked the old man and put the money in his
pocket.

"You'll be all right now, sir."

The old man rested his hand on Michiel's shoulder.

"These potatoes are for my daughter and her two
children. I hope they are still alive when I get back."

"Where do you live?"

"Haarlem." The walk to Haarlem was at least a
hundred miles.

"How old are you, sir?"

"Seventy-eight. God bless you, my son." The man
took up the handle of the cart and shuffled on. Under
this old, wet cap, a fringe of gray hair could be seen.
Michiel stood a moment, watching him. How cruel
the war is, he thought to himself.

That night was not an easy one, either for the ten
hostages or for their wives. The Van Beusekom family
had only four guests—two distant nieces, aged about
thirty, an old ex-Mayor who had studied with Michiel's father, and a real aunt. The guests felt they were
in the way and kept very quiet. Michiel filled the
carbide lamp and then went out to fetch the milk.
Suddenly he realized that he had forgotten to take any
food to Jack and that he had not been there the day
before either. It was too late to go now, because he

would not be back before eight. He did not want to add to his mother's worries. He was annoyed with himself. To share his troubles with someone, he whispered to Erica, "I forgot to go to Jack."

"Never mind," Erica replied under her breath.

"Why?"

"I took him something to eat."

Michiel thought, Blast Erica, she just goes her own way.

"Did you tell him about Father?" he asked.

"No, he has enough troubles as it is. His wound is getting worse. It is too cold and too damp in that hideout. He does not look well."

Michiel thought the risk of Erica visiting Jack was beginning to be too great. A girl going into the woods looked too obvious. But what could he do? It was his own fault. He was the one who had told her.

However, he just couldn't concentrate on the problem of Jack. This other matter dominated all his thoughts. He looked at the clock: ten to nine. He noticed that his mother could not sit still; she was constantly getting up to do some trivial thing, like moving a vase, straightening a chair, or something equally unnecessary. At a quarter past nine the guests went to bed. Erica had managed to control herself until that moment, but now she started to cry, her head against her mother's shoulder. Her mother stroked her hair, but was unable to speak. Without realizing it, Michiel started splitting up the kindling.

"What's the time?" his mother asked.

"A quarter to ten," Michiel answered.

Erica went to make them all another cup of coffee.

"I wish I were Jochem," Michiel said. Jochem had been peacefully asleep for hours.

"The things your father must be going through!" Mrs. Van Beusekom whispered.

"Father and the nine others."

"Do you think he'll pray?" Erica asked, when she came back with the coffee.

Mother nodded slowly.

"I think even the most stubborn unbeliever would pray in such circumstances. I certainly do."

"So do I," said Erica.

Michiel was silent. To be honest, he had not thought of praying. He had been thinking of all sorts of wild possibilities, or rather impossibilities, of rescuing his father. He imagined himself dressing up in a German uniform and entering the barracks. He would go straight up to the commandant with a gun, push it against his temple and force him to pick up the phone and order the prisoners' immediate release. If only he had a German uniform and a gun! But even then . . . Oh, it was nonsense. He could not do anything. If only Uncle Ben had been here! Perhaps he would have thought of a good plan. But how could he find Uncle Ben? And before tomorrow morning? One was not allowed out after eight and the only telephones were the ones the Germans had. In any case, nobody ever knew where Uncle Ben was, so it was impossible.

Should he pray? He would rather have been doing something practical. Was praying the same as taking action, or not? He looked at his mother and Erica,

who were both sitting and staring into the fire, their
hands in their laps. He tried to concentrate on what
he had learned at Sunday school. The trees in the
marketplace were in between him and God. How
would they do it? Would his father have to climb onto
a little box, which they would drag away from under
his feet?

It was just not possible; God would not let it
happen. So, what had he left to pray about? Michiel
got up and went to the back door to look out. The sky
had cleared. The stars shed their cold, impersonal
light. Suddenly he saw a falling star and wished: "My
father safe at home."

Could the soldier have been hit by a falling tree? Or
by lightning? Perhaps he had had a heart attack. No,
that was not possible. His skull had been damaged.
But the falling tree was a possibility. Would the
commander think of it? Michiel ran up to his little
room as quickly as possible. He lit a candle and looked
for a piece of paper. Then, in his best German (which
was none too good), he wrote:

Sir,
    You have informed us that you are going to hang ten people
tomorrow morning if the murderer of the German soldier has
not surrendered by then. Could the soldier not have been hit
by a falling tree? There was a terrible thunderstorm some six
weeks ago. Perhaps a tree was struck by lightning and fell on
him. Will you please give us time to sort this out?
                                        Respectfully,
                                        Michiel Van Beusekom

He folded the letter, put it in an envelope, and slipped through the darkness to their neighbors, the Knoppers. The living room window was blacked out with dark paper. He tapped on the pane. A moment later, the front door opened a crack and Mrs. Knopper whispered, "Dirk?"

"No, no. It's me," said Michiel.

"Oh, it's you." There was disappointment in the voice. "I thought for a moment . . ."

"Oh, I'm so sorry."

"Oh no, my boy. We are all in terrible trouble at the moment. What can I do for you?"

"I have a letter for the commander of the barracks and you have officers in the house. Could you ask them to take the letter with them?"

"I don't know." Mrs. Knopper hesitated. "When must the letter be there?"

"Before tomorrow morning. Before they . . ."

"Well, give it to me, I'll try. Just wait a minute . . ." She vanished upstairs. Michiel heard voices above and then she came down.

"He'll do it. He is going to the barracks at six o'clock in the morning."

"Thank you, Mrs. Knopper. Any news from Dirk?"

"Not a word."

"Good night."

"Sleep well, Michiel."

"Where have you been?" Mrs. Van Beusekom asked when he returned. When Michiel told her what he had done, his mother stroked his hair. "I pray it will help. Come along, children, let's try to get some sleep."

"Impossible," said Erica.

"Well, we might as well lie down and at least rest a little." They went up to their rooms. They each lay in bed, staring wide-eyed into the darkness.

The rumor must have come from Zwanenburg, whose farm was quite near the barracks. He had told the milkman and the milkman had told everyone he had met on his round as he collected churns. Soon the whole village knew. At half past six that morning there had been shooting at the barracks; many simultaneous shots, as if a firing squad were carrying out an execution. Michiel, his mother, and Erica walked around with taut faces. They were white from the lack of sleep and strain. Moreover, they had also heard the rumors.

"I'll go to the barracks again," said Mrs. Van Beusekom. "I must make sure."

But it was not necessary.

Before she left, at eight o'clock, soldiers had put up a notice on the wall of the church. It said that that morning four of the hostages had been shot. If by next morning the culprit had not turned up, the other six would die. The four unlucky persons were the village secretary, the vet, the headmaster, and a city gentleman who had retired to Vlank. The wives of these men received letters covered with many stamps and informing them that their husbands were dead. German Army administration was very efficient—and not only in that. The bodies were brought home in coffins. One could almost hear the menacing, rumbling threat, the repressed cry of rage, that might explode at any moment. No German dared walk on the streets and, in particular, the traitorous National Socialists kept well out of sight. The families of the six remaining hostages were paralyzed with fear. They were exhausted and unable to think properly.

Every day must pass as did that twenty-third of November, 1944. The Van Beusekoms had another sleepless night, save for a few moments of unconsciousness caused by utter fatigue. At half past six, Michiel got up. He drew back the dark, paper blackout curtains. It was barely light, and he could see the street. As he lit the stove, he looked out several times. Suddenly, he noticed a small group of men plodding along, dark silhouettes in the scanty light. The one in front was walking bent almost double, but . . . surely it was the wealthy Mr. Schilthuis, one of the ten hostages?

Michiel dashed out of the house toward them. It was Schilthuis and the notary, and the tax inspector . . . but where was his father?

"Where is my father?" he cried, grabbing Schilthuis's arm.

"Boy, you scared me. Who are you?"

"It's Michiel, the Mayor's son," said notary Van der Hoeven slowly.

"The Mayor's son?"

Why did Schilthuis say that in such a low voice?

"Why is my father not with you?"

Michiel's voice was sharp with anger.

"They shot him, just an hour ago. We five could go home, but they shot him, the murderers."

Michiel dropped Schilthuis's arm. Without a word, he turned round and went toward the house. His mother and Erica had heard the sound of voices and came up to him, their eyes wide with fear.

———

The Germans realized that the people were simmering with outrage, and had calculated that if they shot all six hostages the whole village would boil with anger. So they decided to release five to placate the people. But they shot the Mayor whom they did not trust anyway, to save face. The fact that this Mayor had a family, that he had a little six-year-old son who would be left fatherless, was of no consequence. War was war.

Chapter 7

A week had passed since the burial. Michiel's eyes seemed darker. He had lost weight and his face now had a look of grim determination. He felt himself the head of the family, though his mother was there and Erica was older. Oddly enough, he now felt less afraid of the Germans than before. He bent all his efforts toward helping to bring about an end to this horrible war by outwitting the Germans. He would risk no one's life, however, and that clearly precluded any direct attack on soldiers or German property. Instead, he gave his time to helping those who were hunted or persecuted by the enemy. In particular, he was determined to see Jack successfully through the war.

It was during that week after his father's burial that

he visited the hideout. As usual, he prowled carefully through the trees. But when he came to the entrance the pilot was not there to greet him. That had never happened before. Jack always heard him, even though he moved very quietly.

"Psst," he said.

No answer. What was wrong? Had Jack been caught? Was Michiel walking into a trap? Stealthily he peeped inside. To his relief, but also to his extreme annoyance, he saw Jack and his sister kissing, blissfully unaware of possible danger.

"What's the matter with you?" Jack was asking in a soft voice. "You look so pale and sad lately."

"Oh, nothing special. You needn't worry." And she added, "You are a darling." Then the kissing started again.

"Hm!" Michiel coughed. "I have the feeling that I am interrupting something."

The two lovers jumped.

"Watchfulness is more important than a girl," Michiel said, as if he was much older than the two of them.

"I apologize," Jack grinned. "You see, we're in love."

"So it seems," Michiel said dryly. "About the most stupid thing I have done in this war was to bring Erica here."

"Why? Am I not permitted to love him? What do you have against him?"

"I have nothing against him, but I object to your sending the three of us the same way as our father."

"What's happened to your father?"

"He was shot last week as a reprisal victim," Michiel said.

Jack was stunned. "Shot? How terrible! Last week? My darling, that was why you were so sad." He drew Erica toward him.

Michiel was troubled by this new development, but he had learned enough of life by now to know that no matter what he said or did, Erica would still visit Jack.

"Well," he said, "*you* had better bring Jack his food."

That was too much for Erica. "You brat, are you forgetting I'm older than you? You're not my master, it's the other way around."

"Oh yes? And who takes the responsibility?"

"He's right, darling; as long as Dirk is in prison, he is the head of his little resistance group."

"All right, then," Michiel said. "You come twice a week and I'll come once, but you must promise to be very careful—in fact, you will do exactly as I say. You will enter the woods in a different place each time, and so on."

"I think you are exaggerating the dangers, but all right, I'll do as you say."

"Good girl," said Jack.

After that, Jack and Erica looked as if they could do without Michiel's presence, so he quickly crawled away on his stomach.

———

It was a Sunday. Michiel stood looking out of the

window. The stream of refugees had ceased. The road was empty. The family had been very subdued since that Thursday. Nobody seemed to want to talk, only Jochem chattered away. A sharp-eared person might have picked up the faint droning in the distance. It gradually grew louder, until the bombers swept overhead on their way to unload their destruction on the German towns.

"Good for them," Michiel grunted. "I hope they don't miss."

"But think of all those women and child . . . " his mother started. Then she hesitated.

Did she remember the discussion they had had with their father?

"Well, they began it," he had said. "Serves them right." Did she not feel revengeful now? Did she not feel the hardening of her heart?

"Hey, look!" Michiel exclaimed. They all rushed to the window and looked out. Far off, about half a mile away, the road was crowded with people, like a river of ants, which every now and then sent off little tributaries to the gates of the front gardens. The gardens were filled with people coming out of their houses.

"What's happening?"

The group came nearer. The Van Beusekoms went outside to see what it was all about. Men, thousands of them, in rows of five and six, were walking in their direction. They carried suitcases and bags. Many soldiers, guns on their shoulders, were swarming around trying to keep control. But they could not prevent the men running over to the gardens and taking the food that was offered to them.

"Those people are starving!" Mrs. Van Beusekom cried. "Look how they snatch at the bread. Did you see that one, the tall one with the green shawl? He took a piece of bread out of the mud and swallowed it."

"Why are these people so hungry, Mama?" Jochem asked.

"I don't know. Come on, let's see what we have in the house. We can do without food for today."

So they went into the house, cut up what bread they had, brought apples from the attic, milk from the cellar, divided two bolognas in slices as quickly as they could, and rushed out of the house again. The column of people had reached their house and was passing by. When they saw the food, men rushed up to them. In the wink of an eye, everything had disappeared.

"Where do you all come from?" Michiel asked a boy who was no more than two years his senior.

"From Rotterdam—police raid. They just took every man they could find. 'Off you go, to Germany to work in the factories,' they said."

"Get going!" a German shouted, and the boy disappeared into the crowd.

"How far is it to the barracks from here?" an old man asked.

"A mile and a half."

"So far?"

"That's not far!"

"We have come from Rotterdam, four days' walking and nothing to eat. I am finished. I won't get there. I have a stomach ulcer." All the same, he tramped on, clutching his cane suitcase.

Many people escaped in the village. They jumped behind trees, hid among the people who had lined the roadside to watch, or jumped into the foxholes. Mr. Koster, the forester, who had long been living in the village, devised a new game. He snatched away someone's suitcase and hissed in his ear, "Come and stand next to me and look innocent." One of the guards approached him because he was holding a suitcase.

"What do you want? I live here. Or didn't you think we had suitcases too?" he snarled at the German. There was no time to sort the matter out, so it was dropped. Mr. Koster sent the man into the house with his suitcase and selected the next victim for his liberation act. In this way he succeeded in extracting five people from the crowd: not a bad score, really.

Six thousand men and boys passed by, exhausted by the long march. They disappeared into the barracks near the railway to pass the night. As it turned out, they were to stay there for several days.

That night, Michiel awoke, thinking he heard something in the house. Was it imagination? It was quiet again. Then he heard a door close very softly. It must be his mother or Erica awake. He turned on his other side and tried to go to sleep. But he could not. He felt something was happening. Burglars? You're supposed to be the man of the house, he told himself. Screwing up his courage, he got out of bed. Quickly and noiselessly he went downstairs, hopping over the third step, which had a creak. Then he stood still and listened. He heard a soft murmur in the living room. With his heart in his mouth, but without hesitating, he threw open the door.

The room was lit by four candles. Two strangers, one young man and one old, were seated by the table. His mother squatted on the floor tending the feet of the old man. Michiel saw at a glance that the skin was raw and bleeding. The men had started when the door opened. The younger one got up to leave by the garden exit. The older one simply stiffened with fear.

"Calm down, gentlemen," Michiel's mother said. "This is my eldest son. He is no friend to the Germans."

"Certainly not," Michiel whispered.

"These men escaped from the barracks tonight. They crawled to the village and knocked on our window."

"Very softly," the older man said, as if apologizing. "I'm afraid our presence puts you in great danger."

"Not really. It seems to me, you're workers, not political prisoners," Michiel's mother said.

The men were silent.

"Was it difficult to get away?" Michiel asked.

"Well, you see, there were too many prisoners and too few guards. There was no barbed wire, just a fence around the camp. All the same, our German friends have other methods of dissuading you from escape.

At the end of the afternoon a man got away over the fence. His luck was out and he ran straight into the arms of a patrol. You know what they did? They gave him a spade and made him dig a hole, just outside the camp where we could all see what was happening. When it was finished, he had to lie down on the edge. The officer drew his revolver and shot him in the neck, quite casually, as if he was treading on an ant. With his boot, he pushed him into the hole and ordered two of us to cover it. 'That is what we do to people who don't like our hospitality,' he said, swinging a cane."

Mrs. Van Beusekom wiped her eyes with the back of her hand.

"And you dared to escape, just the same?" Michiel asked.

"In the night, when it was dark. It was easy to climb the fence," the younger man replied.

"For you, perhaps, but what about your . . . well, is this your father?"

"Yes, indeed. Sorry, I did not introduce myself. My name is de Groot, and this is my son David."

"I am Mrs. Van Beusekom, and Michiel is my son."

"Pleased to meet you."

"It was not easy for my father to climb the fence, but he managed."

"You took a great risk," Mrs. Van Beusekom remarked thoughtfully. "Was it so important for you to get away, that you risked your life?"

Michiel looked closely at the two men. They were

rather small. The boy was dark and his father gray, and he had detected a trace of an accent when the father spoke.

Mrs. Van Beusekom cleared away her plasters and bandage.

"Now you'll be able to manage better, Mr. Polak, er . . . de Groot, I mean."

Both men flushed. Michiel also went red. Polak is a common Jewish name. Apparently, his mother had realized they were Jews and made the mistake intentionally. She was right. The men looked Jewish and it explained why they had dared to escape. They simply had to. There was no telling what would have happened had the Germans discovered them.

The elderly man looked helplessly at Mrs. Van Beusekom.

"So you realized," he stammered.

"That was not so difficult. You don't exactly look as if you were called de Groot."

"Our name is Kleerkoper. We shall leave immediately. We put you in great danger. Come on, David."

They got up and walked to the door.

"And where were you thinking of going, Mr. Kleerkoper?" Michiel's mother asked very calmly.

"To Overyssel. We know a family there with the name de Groot who will hide us."

"And how were you going to cross the river? Every bridge, every ferry, is controlled by the Germans."

"Well, I don't know," Mr. Kleerkoper said, and he looked uncertain. "We'll find a way, I guess."

"Well, let's think it over together. Four heads are

better than two. But first, please explain how you could have been caught out in the open. Are there still Jews walking in the streets after nearly five years of the occupation? I thought every single Jew was either in a concentration camp or hidden in an attic or a cellar."

"Well, it was an unfortunate coincidence," Mr. Kleerkoper said. "But if you are interested I'll tell you."

"Please do. It is half past three, and we have time to listen." Mr. Kleerkoper sat down and told his tragic story:

———

"I was born in Germany in 1890. Our family name was Rosenthal. We felt German and were treated no differently because of our Jewishness. Our friends and neighbors included not only other Jews, but Catholics and all kinds of Protestants.

"When I served in the German Army in the last war they even gave me the Iron Cross—the highest military award given to anyone.

"After the war, I met and later married Lotte Kleerkoper, a Dutch girl from a Jewish family. Even though we made our home in Germany, I learned Dutch to please my wife. We always spoke it together—so our children, David and Rosemary, grew up learning Dutch as well as German.

"The rise of Hitler took place when the children were still at primary school. That was in the 'thirties. At first, we only knew about anti-Semitism through the newspapers: when anything went wrong, the Jews were always blamed. Little by little, it began to affect our daily lives. Our servant had to leave because no young Aryan woman could work in a Jewish household with men; our children had to use a special door in the school—that was before they had to stay away altogether; my wife found the grocer and other tradespeople less willing to serve her. As for me, as long as people still wanted to buy furniture from me, they were at least polite.

"I kept thinking that the Germans, who had always accepted us, would change their attitude back to what it had been before. I only gave up hope in 1938. That was the year Jews had to register all their property—this could only mean that the Nazis intended to take over everything belonging to the Jews. The so-called 'Crystal Night,' when Jewish property was actually attacked, made me decide to leave my homeland forever. I could no longer make a living, as my furniture store had been completely vandalized—the windows were smashed, every stick of furniture was broken, fabrics were ripped to pieces—and there was nothing fit to sell.

"We probably would have stayed in spite of this if our friends and neighbors had protested or showed sympathy with our loss, but no one ever said a kind word to us. It was then we realized that our position was hopeless.

"We came to Holland to live. I was so bitter and disillusioned about my country that I even put away my name and took my wife's. So our new life began under a new name: Kleerkoper.

"We thought we had finished with Germany, but on the tenth of May, 1940 the Germans entered Holland and continued their persecuting. We were not allowed on the trains, in buses, or in cinemas. We had to wear a yellow star with a 'J' on it on our coats. Many were arrested and sent to concentration camps, and others were just slaughtered like cattle. One could only whisper about it. Why? Because we were Jews; that was the only reason. It was beyond comprehension.

"Fortunately, many Dutch non-Jews were willing to hide us. I arranged for my family to live in the attic of a friend—Mr. Voerman. But it was already too late. One Monday night, just after David and I had gone to make final arrangements with the Voerman family, the Germans raided our house and took away Lotte and Rosemary. I had no illusions: there was hardly a chance that I would ever see them again. And so it was just David and me who went to live in Voerman's attic. By this time my hair had turned as gray as ashes.

"The Germans had the unpleasant practice of coming quite suddenly during the night to search houses for hidden Jews. About a week ago they came to Voerman's. Even from the attic I heard the noise of boots kicking at the door. Then I heard German voices and my host saying he had nothing to hide. I knew we were sure to be found and decided on a desperate plan. I put on my dressing gown and slippers and went downstairs. Standing on the staircase, I began shouting in German. Since I had been a German soldier myself, I knew how an officer would behave.

"'What's all this noise in the middle of the night?' I yelled. 'Don't you know that Colonel von Brandenburg has a room in this house? These are his quarters! Would you please get it into your thick skulls that this is Colonel von Brandenburg standing in front of you! While shouting this, I had entered the room. The sergeant in charge of the group started to answer, but I didn't give him a chance.

"'Why didn't you tell these people right away I was quartered here?' I shrieked at Voerman.

"'I'm sorry, Herr Colonel,' Voerman said in a subdued voice. 'I was so upset by the noise they made and I was just dozing off, if you see what I mean. I . . .'

"'*Unverschämt!*' I barked. 'Disgraceful! What is your name, Sergeant?'

The sergeant clicked his heels and said, 'Sergeant Mayer, Third Battalion, sir.'

"'You will hear from me, Sergeant Mayer. You may leave. *Heil Hitler!*'

Sergeant Mayer clicked his heels again. "'Yes, Herr Colonel. *Heil Hitler!*'

"He left with his men. Voerman and I shook hands silently, knowing that we had just missed concentration camp.

"'You were marvelous, Jitzchak.'

"'But now we'll all have to disappear,' I said. 'I'm sorry. We must get away tomorrow morning—you, your wife, David, and me. That sergeant is bound to ask if anyone has ever heard of the short-tempered Colonel von Brandenburg. Where are we all going to hide?'

"Voerman knew someone who provided addresses for all of us. He and his wife went to Overyssel, to a family called de Groot. But the journey would have been too dangerous for David and me. We got an address in Kralingen, a suburb of Rotterdam. It was dangerous enough to get there, but we had a reasonable chance of making it.

"'If you happen to be near, do visit us,' Voerman said. 'The de Groot family are farmers with golden hearts; they are sure to find a place for you. Now, my dear friends, take care and do your best to come through the war alive. I'm sorry you have to move.'

"I thanked him for everything and said, 'As for the moving, better a wandering Jew than a heel-clicking German.'

"Then we walked straight out into the arms of a special patrol. The raiding soldiers never even looked at our papers. They simply took everyone they saw. Some were allowed to pack up a few things under supervision. But as David and I were already carrying our suitcases, we were marched off to Vlank. On the road there had been no chances to escape, because the guards seemed to be keeping an eye on us. Did they

sense something? We didn't know. We had to wait
until we were in the barracks, and succeeded in the
end. But how long will we stay free?"

"Till the end of the war, I hope," Michiel's mother
said. "We'll have to devise a foolproof plan to get you
over the river."

"We could dress you up as farmers' wives, in local
dress," Michiel suggested. "A white headscarf, wide
skirts, a bodice, and there you are."

"It can't be done at the river Yssel. They control
papers too strictly."

"Well, I only meant this for traveling along the
roads," Michiel said. "We must certainly think of
something else for crossing the river. Wait a minute, that suddenly reminds me about the Koppel
ferry. . . ."

"Why?"

"The other day I heard an intriguing story about
the Koppel ferry. If it's true, we'll be able to get these
gentlemen over on the ferryboat without any difficulty. I'll go and find out as soon as possible."

Mr. Kleerkoper peered over his steel spectacles.
"You have a very energetic son, indeed, madam.
You must know what risks he runs, but does *he*?"

Mrs. Van Beusekom put her hand on Michiel's arm
and said, "There was a time when I did not want my
children to take any action against the occupying
forces. I considered it too dangerous and thought it
made little difference. I must say, I never really
expected Michiel to follow my wishes, but ever since
he stopped going to school I have had no idea of what

he was doing. I didn't like it, but what could I do? In times of war a boy of sixteen is an adult, isn't he? However, a few weeks ago I changed my point of view. I told you that my husband died: I did not tell you that the Germans shot him in cold blood, as a reprisal victim."

Her voice did not falter while she was saying this and she showed not one tear of emotion, only a slight flush showed on her face. She went on fiercely. "Michiel and I have not spoken about it to each other, but I know that we two, and also my daughter Erica, will do everything we possibly can against the murderers. So I gladly permit my son . . . oh well, nowadays mothers don't actually *permit* teenage sons to do anything, that is old-fashioned. I just think that one must do one's utmost to keep people out of the claws of those vultures who want to make one big graveyard out of Europe."

"Amen," said Mr. Kleerkoper respectfully.

Chapter 8

Near the Koppel ferry there stood a large white house. It was the property of Baroness Weddik Wansfeld, a thin, dignified lady of over sixty. She lived in the house with her daughter, her son-in-law, a brother of her late husband, two unmarried nieces, a butler, and two maidservants. In spite of the presence of several men, there was no doubt as to who was master of the house—the dowager Louise Adelheid Mathilde Bella, Baroness Weddik Wansfeld. Needless to say, because of her initials, she was often called "Lamb" behind her back. It was a decidedly unsuitable name, since she was quite the opposite of a lamb.

Very much against her will, she had been forced to

quarter the five soldiers who controlled the ferry day
and night. The guard was changed every week. It was
by order of the garrison commander that they were
billeted in the large white house. The Baroness object-
ed vehemently and put up such a fight that the
commander had to visit her personally to achieve his
aim.

"Well," she said in impeccable German, "they may
come, but they must adhere strictly to the rules of the
house."

"Of course, m'lady," the commander said, with all
that respect that a German military officer has for the
gentry. "Our soldiers are well disciplined and they'll
behave themselves. I will vouch for that."

And so the dowager had laid down her rules. The
other residents of the house were strictly forbidden to
talk to the soldiers. Even if it concerned only a broken
cup, the Baroness alone would handle the matter. As
for the soldiers, there were many rules. They were
not written down, so the commander did not know
them. Every Monday morning, after the changing of
the guard, the new soldiers had to report to the
Baroness in her rooms. She would sit very straight in
her chair, while the men stood to attention. Then she
would repeat the rules, permitting no interruption.
The sergeant had to sleep in the house, the soldiers in
the stables. There was to be no noise after ten at
night. All refuse was to be placed in the bin outside
the kitchen.

"Between three and half past, tea is served on the

veranda. My staffing does not allow for shifts, so I expect you all to be there at three o'clock sharp. The veranda is large enough."

And so she went on. She had such a commanding manner, and so great was the soldiers' respect for authority, that every new group walked into the trap. Tea on the veranda from three to half past three—that seemed to be the custom, so during that period the ferry was unguarded, and some people knew this. The word was passed on in whispers to those who could be trusted. Every day Van Dyk, the ferryman, had a boatload of people who had no identification cards, or who had something to hide, or who did not want to be seen, while Louise Adelheid Mathilde Bella (Lamb), Baroness Weddik Wansfeld, conversed with the German guards.

———

Next morning, at nine, Michiel was announced to the Baroness. She received him graciously. She expressed her sorrow at the death of his father, and openly showed her disgust at the German methods.

"What can I do for you, young man?"

"Information, please, madam. As you live so near the ferry, I wondered if you could tell me whether there is a boat between three and half past? I want to get two farmers' wives to the other side."

"Two farmers' wives?" the Baroness repeated. "How old are you?"

"Almost sixteen, madam."

"You should be at school."

"There is no transport to Zwolle and my bicycle is in no condition to . . ."

"I see, but you can give lifts to farmers' wives? On the back of your bicycle?"

"I hope to borrow a horse-and-cart from Van Coenen."

"And what if he refuses?"

Michiel said nothing. What *could* he say?

"Why can't these farmers' wives go across the bridge?"

"They like going by boat best," Michiel said. He did not want to reveal his secret, but on the other hand he did not want to be rude to the Baroness.

"And why between three and half past?"

"Well, it's teatime then, and they hope to get a cup of tea on board."

"What are their names?"

"Eh, well . . . what was their name, now? Bartel, I believe. Mrs. Bartel and her daughter Antje."

"And why are you taking them?"

"Well, somebody has to take them. Moreover, their name begins with B and so does mine."

"Are you trying to make fun of me, young man?"

"Oh no, m'lady. How could you possibly think such a thing?"

The Baroness's lean face betrayed a faint smile.

"Very well, be at the barn at half past one. There you will find my tilbury and Caesar. I take it that you can handle horses? At five minutes past three the ferryboat leaves. I will expect the tilbury to be back by seven."

"Thank you so much, it is extremely . . ."

The regal old lady stood up. The interview was over, and she dismissed Michiel with a nod of her head. He left the room as quickly as he could, full of admiration for this extraordinary woman.

Jitzchak and his son shaved carefully. Then their faces were powdered to hide their dark stubble. Their dresses had come from a farmer's wife in the neighborhood, and Erica and her mother had altered them to fit. The white headscarves were a particularly effective part of the disguise. The two of them made quite a picture, standing side by side in their rural dress.

"Catch!" Mrs. Van Beusekom called, throwing an apple to Mr. Kleerkoper. Instinctively, he put his knees together, as men do when they are wearing trousers.

"Wrong." Mrs. Van Beusekom smiled. "A woman in a long, wide skirt would open her knees, to catch the apple in her lap."

Dave grinned. "You're not much good as a woman, Father."

"Maybe not," Mr. Kleerkoper said, "but are you any better?" He was busy rolling a cigarette of home-grown tobacco and he threw it to David, who, having been forewarned, spread his knees and caught the cigarette in his skirt.

"Before you start getting too confident, show us how a woman strikes a match," said his father.

"I know—a man strikes toward himself, with his middle finger just behind the head of the match—

look, like that. But a woman holds the match further down and strikes it away from her." He struck the match with what he supposed to be a woman's mannerisms, and lit his cigarette. Then he looked around triumphantly.

"I am very impressed," Mr. Kleerkoper said. "But I've never seen a farmer's wife smoking a cigarette."

Everybody laughed at that, David most of all.

"My father always has the last word," he said.

"We would advise you not to talk on the way, where other people might hear you; not only because you have male voices, but also because you do not speak the local dialect," said Michiel. "Now, I have to be back on this side of the river by seven. That leaves me time to take you quite a bit farther than just the other bank. Where is it that you have to go—or would you prefer not to tell me?"

"The de Groot family live in Den Hulst," Mr. Kleerkoper said.

"That's fifteen miles from Zwolle." Michiel knew that much. "We won't get that far, but we can get quite a distance. Let me see. . . ." He figured it out quickly. "If you have to walk the last five miles you'll still have plenty of time to be there before eight."

"Hadn't we better leave straight away?"

"There's no point. We go on the ferry at five past three."

"Can't we get an earlier one?"

"No, only that one is safe. After the war, I'll tell you why."

"We trust you completely," Mr. Kleerkoper said.

———————

At half past one sharp, Michiel was at the barn by the white house near the river. The tilbury was ready; the fiery black Caesar stamped impatiently on the stones, sending out little sparks. Michiel was apprehensive, but once he was holding the reins, his nervousness gave way to a kind of recklessness. The horse trotted briskly, straight along the country road. He responded perfectly to each touch of the reins, and gave the impression that he could win a race for thoroughbreds without any training at all. Michiel had often handled horses when helping the farmers with the harvest, but they had plodded slowly, pulling heavily laden wagons. This was something much better. Sitting on the tilbury, which carried his two make-believe farmers' wives, he felt like a hero, a sort of Ben Hur; especially when Mr. Kleerkoper clung anxiously to the bench and David said admiringly that he seemed to be an old hand with horses.

All too soon, much of his pleasure vanished, for suddenly he saw Schafter up ahead. He was on foot, and as the tilbury passed, he put up his hand to ask for a lift. Michiel had only a few seconds in which to decide. Schafter beside him on the driving seat, asking questions? Never! So he pretended not to see him. Out of the corner of his eye, Michiel saw Schafter's surprised glance at the passengers. No doubt he was asking himself who they might be, for he knew everyone in the neighborhood. He would also be curious to know where the mayor's son could be taking these two women. Yes, to the ferry, of course. Schafter was not stupid.

Anyway, he won't make the three o'clock ferry, so what does it matter? I can tell him some story or other later, Michiel thought hurriedly.

Everything went well. The crossing was no problem. There was not a German in sight. Michiel asked the ferryman if he could return at half past six.

"That's the Baroness's horse," Van Dyk remarked.

Michiel nodded. He expected Van Dyk to ask more, but he was silent. They met no difficulties on the other side either, and drove on for more than an hour at a brisk trot. Then Michiel said, "I think I'd better turn back here. I want to be in plenty of time. You never know what might happen. Also, it looks as if Caesar would like to go a little slower. You think you can find your way now?"

"Certainly," Mr. Kleerkoper said.

He and Dave got down and shook hands with Michiel.

"God bless you, my boy!" His words were the same as those of the old man with the broken wheel. What else was there to say?

"Now that we've gone, you'll be out of danger," Dave said.

"I do hope we'll meet again. Good-bye." Michiel turned the tilbury around. He thought the way back would not be much of a problem, either—but he was wrong!

He had been driving for only about twenty minutes when he saw another horse-and-cart coming toward him from a side path. It was an ordinary flat cart, such as farmers use to carry their hay or rye. But the unusual thing was the two armed German soldiers sitting on top and four horses tied on behind. Michiel knew only too well what that meant: horse *razzia*, sent out to commandeer horses.

The cart reached the main road about a quarter of a mile behind him. Michiel immediately started to use the whip. The horse was by no means exhausted and sped on as fast as it could.

"*Halt!*" Michiel heard them calling. What should he do? He looked around and saw the German driver also using his whip. If he stopped, the Baroness would lose Caesar. She would receive a slip of paper saying that the German nation owned her one horse. That would not be too dreadful, but they would also ask him questions. What was he doing here? He felt the nerves in his stomach tightening, but at the same time his face grew angry and taut, as it had been at the time of his father's burial. "Come on, Caesar!"

He heard them calling again. Their own horse could not keep pace with the Baroness's fiery black stallion and they knew they were losing him. All the more reason for wanting to claim the horse. One of the soldiers raised his gun and fired a shot into the air. Michiel realized that he was not far enough ahead to be out of range. Then he noticed a small path to the right. In full flight he swung the tilbury onto it. It all but tipped over. The path led to the woods and many carts seemed to use it. He noticed tracks leading off to the left and right. Could he deceive his pursuers?

Ahead, he suddenly noticed some farmers cutting wood and loading it onto carts, which explained the tracks on the path. He could hear the cries of the soldiers behind him, though they were still out of sight. He turned to the left, and left again . . . it was a dead end and he had no time to turn back.

"Whoa, Caesar!" Michiel jumped off the box, tied the horse to a tree, and fled into the undergrowth. If they caught him now, it would not be pleasant. Stealthily, he crept forward. He thought he heard voices. Someone was close at hand. Maybe he could trust them and ask for a hiding place? No, better play safe, you could never tell. He crawled forward on his knees. Thank goodness he had been careful. The voices appeared to be those of his pursuers talking to two farmers who had been cutting wood. They were typical Saxon farmers, with tight-fitting blue caps on their heads and a wad of tobacco in each cheek. They took their time about answering the soldiers' questions, thoughtfully chewing their tobacco, scratching their heads, and gazing up to the sky with a bemused expression. In short, they gave the Germans the impression that they were not much more intelligent than their pigs.

"Well, did you see him or not?" one of the Germans barked.

"Was that a black horse that passed by just now, Dirk?" one of the farmers asked.

"A black horse? Aye, might have been," the other man replied.

"You mentioned a cart—did you mean a tilbury?"

"Stop this, you stupid oaf!" The German stamped his foot. "Tell me where the cart went! Which way?"

"Oh, so that's what you want to know, sir, is it? Oh, well, now, let me see . . . to the right," and he pointed in the opposite direction to the one Michiel had taken. The Germans were suspicious. Was the man speaking the truth? The farmer gave them a childish, innocent grin, such as only a Saxon farmer can do.

"Oh yes, Mr. Soldier, sir, that's the way it went. To the right."

"Right, come on, then." And they disappeared along the right-hand path.

Michiel ran back to his horse, jumped onto the box, and drove back as quickly as he could. As he passed the woodcutters, he stopped and called out, "Did you send them in the wrong direction?" The two men grinned and one pointed in the direction that the Germans had gone.

"They are following a black horse."

"Thank you. 'Bye."

"Good-bye."

A few minutes later, Michiel was back on the road and went on his way to the Koppel ferry. He got there just before half past six. Van Dyk took him to the other side of the river and he returned the horse and tilbury to the white house. He wanted to thank the Baroness but she was nowhere to be seen. Then he cycled home quickly.

As he went up the garden path, he thought he noticed his mother watching out for him. Whether she was or not, she did not want him to know, because she was busy in the kitchen when he entered the house, and she just asked in a calm voice if everything had gone well.

"Fine!" said Michiel. "Only, on the way back some of our friends wanted to take the horse and gave chase. They even opened fire. Only in the air," he added, seeing the frightened look on his mother's face. "It was easy to get away. That Caesar is a wonderful horse."

"Good," his mother said, trying to sound as casual as possible. "Shall I make you something to eat?"

Even so, she could not help kissing the back of his head as he passed.

———

Just before eight o'clock, Uncle Ben appeared. He had not seen them for weeks, and knew nothing about the death of Michiel's father.

"If only I had been here, perhaps I could have done something . . ."

"Well, what could you have done?" Michiel asked.

"A raid on the barracks, or . . . well, I suppose it would have been impossible. Do *you* know who killed the German in the woods?"

"No, of course not. That person's not going to show up. He prefers to let five men be shot."

"It's awful," Uncle Ben remarked.

To cheer his uncle up, Michiel told him about the escape of Mr. Kleerkoper and his son, the journey to the other side of the river, and the pursuit by the soldiers. Uncle Ben slapped him on the shoulder—just a little harder than Michiel would have liked!

"Good for you, boy. If the war lasts another year, you'll be able to join the resistance movement."

It was quite an effort for Michiel not to tell him that he was already involved in resistance activities.

———

Later, in the middle of the night, Michiel was wakened by the sound of Allied airplanes. A Spitfire passed, low, over the roof of the house, two or three times. It was a sound that made your heart stop beating and you wanted to run away as fast as you could. Rinus de Raadt, maybe, he thought.

Michiel could not get back to sleep. He thought about Schafter. What could he tell him? The man was bound to question him until he knew every detail. It was only after he had thought up a really good story for Schafter that he fell asleep again.

Chapter 9

The next morning, Michiel decided to take a casual stroll past Schafter's house in the hope of meeting him. On his way, he met Mr. Postma. His first reaction was to turn away. He was sure Mr. Postma was part of the resistance group in Vlank, and he held them responsible for his father's death. Mr. Postma noticed that Michiel looked away from him, so he walked up, and grasping the buttons of his overcoat, he said, "I know I should not say this—but, Michiel, you must know that the resistance group in Vlank does not know who killed the soldier in the wood. I'm sure of that."

Michiel immediately felt ashamed.

"Thank you, sir," he stammered.

"Will you please forget that I told you this?"

"I've already forgotten."

"Good for you."

They went their separate ways and Michiel walked past Schafter's house. There was no one in sight, so he went on a little farther and then turned around to go home. As he passed the house for the second time, he saw Schafter in his front garden.

"'Morning, Mr. Schafter."

"Hello, Michiel. Didn't you want to see me yesterday?"

"Me? Where? When?"

"On the road to the ferry. You passed me going like the wind, in the Baroness's tilbury. It *was* her tilbury, wasn't it?"

"Yes, it was."

"I wanted a lift, but you did not see me."

"I'm sorry."

"Doesn't matter. I had to be at Verheul's, which wasn't that far. I say, those farmers' wives . . ." Schafter came nearer and started to whisper. "Who were they?"

"They were sisters of one of the Baroness's maids," Michiel said. "They are from Uddel, near Elspeet, you know. There was a wedding in Zwolle and the Baroness gave leave for them to go in the tilbury and then Aaltje asked me to drive."

"Why didn't Aaltje go with you?"

"She did."

"But I met her this morning, on this side of the river." Michiel did not know what to say.

"Well, she must have been called back unexpectedly," he stammered.

Schafter gave him a queer look.

"Those sisters, weren't they a couple of men, dressed up?" he asked casually.

"What do you mean? What nonsense!" Michiel tried to sound convincing.

"Oh, I just thought that one of the faces looked rather like a man's."

"Well, I must be going," Michiel said.

"Listen." Schafter came even nearer. "You can trust me. They say I am on the wrong side, but it's not true. I have to transport some people to the other side of the river. If you know a way, please tell me. I'll swear I'll not misuse it."

Michiel shivered. What a sly man this was!

"I don't know what you are talking about. That sort of thing is not my cup of tea. Good-bye!"

Quickly he strode off. He had spoiled everything, everything! What could he do now?

———

That same afternoon the ferryman Van Dyk was arrested and replaced by a stranger. The Baroness was ordered to stay in her house. She was not to leave it till the unsupervised river crossings had been cleared up. It was not known what kind of punishment the ferry guards suffered. In the course of several months, many had fallen into the Baroness's trap. The last sergeant was said to have been demoted. Once again, Michiel expected to be called in for questioning—they would certainly want to know where he had been taking the two women. Once again, he took every care before entering the house. He could hardly eat for nervousness, and had a constant stomach ache. But nothing happened. Nobody seemed to be interested in him. Had Schafter taken pity and not mentioned his name? Michiel could not understand it; he had not been exactly polite to the man. More than ever now, he wished that the liberating armies from Britain, Canada, America, and France might arrive.

After fourteen days the ferry inquiry was closed. They now knew how the Baroness had been involved, and a sergeant went with five men to arrest her. But many weeks passed before Michiel heard what happened after that.

They found the door locked and the shutters closed. The sergeant rang the bell loudly. A small first-floor window opened above them and the Baroness called out, "Go away!"

"I order you to open the door. You are under arrest," the sergeant called back.

"I said, go away . . . a Weddik Wansfeld will never be arrested."

The sergeant did not know what to do. He tried a different approach. "I invite m'lady to come; the garrison commander would like to talk to you."

"That sounds better," the Baroness replied. "My answer is no. If the commander wants to talk to me, he can come here."

"Please, m'lady."

In answer, the window was closed. The sergeant went back to report. What else could he have done? In the afternoon an officer appeared with five men carrying a wooden beam. The scene of that morning was repeated. The bell was rung, the Baroness appeared at an upstairs window.

"If you don't open that door immediately, I'll force it open," the officer shouted. He was a fearsome, brutal man. The men got the beam into position and started to ram the thick front door. A shot was heard and one of the soldiers screamed. He had been hit in the arm.

"*Donnerwetter*," swore the officer. He had caught a glimpse of the Baroness with a gun. "You'll pay for this with your life," he barked.

"That was just a warning. Next time, I aim for a head, *your* head in fact."

"The woman's mad," the officer murmured. It seemed safer to withdraw behind the trees on the other side of the road. Was he going to have to storm this house with six men? That would cost a few lives. Moreover, the commander had told him to treat the lady properly. The commander was the son of an estate steward. He respected the gentry. It really was the limit! One could not sacrifice a few soldiers just to arrest an old woman! He could hurl a few grenades through the windows, but would the commander like that? He decided to go back and report. He could think of nothing better, and was sick of the whole business. Nothing else happened that day, but the following day the commander came himself. He rang the bell gently, and the Baroness appeared at the window on the first floor.

"M'lady, would you be so good as to grant me an interview?" he said.

"Certainly, if you put down your pistol first."

"With pleasure."

The commander undid his belt and holster. A moment later the bolts were drawn back and a chain was unhooked. The door opened. He stepped inside and was confronted by the Baroness, impeccably dressed in a morning gown, with a heavy pistol in her hand. She gestured to him to go into the corridor, and then locked the door behind him, with a heavy bolt and chain.

"Nice pistol," the commander said, sounding more relaxed than he felt. He did not quite like the casual way she was toying with the trigger.

"I also have a revolver and a shotgun, and a lot of ammunition."

"Do you know that the penalty for having weapons in the house is death?" the commander asked.

"Yes, I know. Do come in and sit down. I cannot offer you anything, as my staff is locked in the music room."

"In the music room?"

"Yes, that's right; and so is everyone else who's staying in the house. They are as frightened as mice, so I told them to go into the music room and lock the door."

She *is* mad, the commander thought. She was sitting opposite him, very erect, with her pistol pointing at his heart. He was sure she would shoot, the moment he tried to disarm her.

"M'lady, there is a war on, and I must ask you to come with me."

"Where to?"

"To the barracks."

"To be tried and executed? You have just said I could be put to death for having these weapons. Moreover, I resisted arrest and shot one of your men in the arm. On top of that, you think I have something to do with the ferry affair. My dear commander, I have decided not to be arrested, not even by your *Herrenvolk*."

Despite his admiration for the gentry, the commander was losing his temper.

"Hand me that pistol, madam."

The Baroness tightened her grip on the trigger.

"I'll use force to get you out of this house," he threatened.

"Why didn't you do that yesterday?"

"I had my reasons."

The Baroness rose, indicating that she considered the discussion at an end. Furious, the commander went to the door thinking, I'll snatch the pistol from her at the door, but he did not get a chance. The Baroness inclined her head, indicating that he could open the door himself and take the chains off the hook.

"M'lady, you are acting very unwisely."

Once more, she inclined her head and closed the door behind him.

The next morning, a tank appeared outside the white house. The commander himself was in it. He had been considering the matter all night long and devised a solution that was worthy of any Baroness, not the least this one. He did not leave the tank.

"Baroness," he called, putting his head out. The Baroness appeared at the first-floor window. "Do you surrender?"

"Just a minute."

A moment later, out of a small door at the back of the house, there emerged all the inhabitants, one after the other, like a row of geese: the maids, the butler, the nieces, the brother-in-law, the son-in-law and, lastly, the Baroness's daughter.

"Please come too, Mother," she pleaded.

"To be shot by these rogues in their courtyard at six tomorrow morning? No, thank you, I am too old to be a prisoner, and too proud!"

Her daughter began to cry, and followed the others. The Baroness carefully bolted the door and went up to the balcony, gun in hand.

"Commander!"

"I'm listening, m'lady."

"Will you take note that none of the people in my house have had anything to do with this? They never spoke a word to your soldiers, not one of them. I alone am entirely responsible—no one else."

"I have taken note of the fact," the commander said. "M'lady, will you surrender yourself to me?"

The Baroness took aim and fired. The bullet just missed his head. The commander ducked and closed the hatch cover. The Baroness went back into the house, in her own calm manner, and entered the room where the portraits of her ancestors hung on the walls.

"Fire!" the commander shouted. The tank opened up. Twenty shells landed in the white house, which soon burned like a torch, and the walls collapsed. Only when there was nothing but a burned-out ruin left, in which not a soul could have been alive, did the commander order the tank to leave. As soon as it had disappeared, the Baroness's family, the others who had been living there, and people from the neighborhood, who had all been watching from a distance, began to extinguish the flames.

An hour later they were able to enter what had once been the house. The walls were blackened and holed. After a search they found the Baroness. The Dowager Louise Adelheid Mathilde Bella, Baroness Weddik Wansfeld, was lying under a heap of fallen brickwork. The fire had not reached her. She was wearing an orange scarf. If the commander had taken the trouble to look at her, he would have seen the defiant expression on her face.

Chapter 10

Weeks passed. Months passed. The shortest day, December 21, came and went. Then Christmas 1944, a pitch-black Christmas, and New Year's Eve. Would the New Year bring peace? Everybody wondered. January, a long, cold month with no fuel and little to eat. The hunger in the big cities was worse than ever. Many stomachs were swollen by starvation; hundreds died. Those who could still muster some energy headed eastward and northward in search of a few morsels for their children and the very old people who waited behind. The sad stream of food-gatherers increased, but moved more slowly. People were now very weak.

For Michiel it was a difficult time. The events concerning the Koppel ferry and the Baroness Weddik Wansfeld had shocked him deeply. He had gone to the funeral and discovered that a thousand other people had had the same idea. It was turned into a demonstration of admiration for the Baroness, and a demonstration against the Germans. The garrison commander had sent a wreath, for he wished it to be known that he respected the old lady. Some people had considered it a fine gesture.

Not one of all these people here realizes that it was my fault, Michiel had thought, while he was standing in the cemetery. Not the minister, who was courageous enough to attack the Germans openly in his graveside sermon, nor the new Lady Weddik Wansfeld, who threw flowers on her mother's tomb. Not even the anonymous person who had sent a bunch of flowers tied with orange ribbon, bearing the inscription "Long Live the Queen."

The worst thing was that Michiel didn't know what he had done wrong, neither over Bertus and the letter, nor in this present affair. What else *could* he have done? If he had to take another two Jews across the river Yssel now, would he be able to think of anything better, anything safer? Everything he did went wrong. Because of him, all kinds of people had got into trouble. And yet he was so careful. Was it because he was still a child, and too young for this kind of work? Probably one of these days they would find Jack, too, through his fault. Then the whole miserable story would be complete.

He decided that in future he would have as little as possible to do with secret work, as he obviously wasn't any good at it. Nowadays he went to see Jack only once a week. Erica did the rest and she did it much better than he had expected. To think that he had thought himself so much better than his older sister! How wrong he had been. He was the one who spoiled everything. Should he leave Jack entirely in Erica's hands? No, he didn't have the heart to do that. Dirk had given the letter to him, so it was his responsibility. He doubled his precautions and did his best to anticipate all the mistakes he might make, in order to avoid them. He continued to visit Jack once a week.

Whenever he met Schafter he deliberately looked the other way. By now, the traitor must have realized that he knew who had informed the Germans about the Baroness. It would do him no harm to know what Michiel thought of that, even though he had not revealed Michiel's name to the Germans. If he thought that Michiel was grateful, he was wrong. Michiel was having to carry his cross during this war, and it was not proving a light one.

Erica at last plucked up the courage to remove the plaster from Jack's leg. She would have preferred to have called in the doctor who had treated Jack immediately after he had been hurt, but however much they racked their brains, and however hard Jack tried to remember the name, they could not think who it might have been. Only Dirk knew, and he was a prisoner at Amersfoort. His parents had received a short note telling them.

Erica was concerned about the leg. Where it had been broken there was a large swelling that had become evident only after the plaster had been taken off. Maybe there was nothing extraordinary about it, but it looked as though the bone had mended at a very slight angle. The leg still hurt when Jack tried to walk on it. Nevertheless, he practiced every day and was soon able to get about again. Clearly, though, he was not going to win any sprints in the near future!

The wound on his shoulder was not healing properly, either. Thanks to Erica's good care, at least the infection had cleared up. She changed the bandages twice a week and made sure that the wound was kept completely clean. But it had healed badly.

"What sort of hospital is this?" the semiqualified nurse grumbled. "Bed: a heap of dead leaves. Instruments: a pair of manicure scissors and a small kitchen knife."

"But they are well sterilized," Jack said.

"Yes, that's true," Erica continued, "but they are still hopeless. Food: always stale, never any real fresh vegetables, cold potatoes . . ."

"But cooked with love," Jack said.

"That's also true." Erica smiled, stroking his bearded cheek. "Drinks: cold tea and buttermilk."

"I must admit that I wouldn't mind a whisky," Jack

confessed. He spoke Dutch almost faultlessly now, although he still had a heavy accent.

"Temperature: cold and wet. Rehabilitation center . . ."

"What did you say?"

"Rehabilitation center—room to exercise your broken leg: six feet by six feet, less the space taken up by the aforementioned dry leaves, a rickety chair and a small table. Doctor: absent."

"Other medical help: excellent," Jack said.

"How can I ever give you your health back under these circumstances?"

"Well," said Jack, "just think what I would have to do if I were fit. I'd have to do my best to get back to England, for a start. That's laid down in our Air Force Regulations. Would you like that? Of course, I know I'm rather a burden to you, but . . ."

"No, darling," Erica said, already reconciled to Jack's slow recovery.

It was six-year-old Jochem who created another diversion. He was an enterprising child. One day when Erica and Michiel were out, and his mother busy in the kitchen, he decided to climb onto the roof. To do so, he went to Michiel's room in the attic. That was forbidden, but having made up his mind, Jochem was not going to be put off by such a rule. Once in Michiel's room, he forgot for a while the purpose of his visit. His big brother had so many interesting things to play with. For instance, there was a collection of shells, an old telephone, a roll of flexible electric cord, and an atlas, which lay open at a map of France. Jochem touched everything. He crushed two shells, he drew a new border between France and Germany, as though he were General Eisenhower, Commander-in-Chief of the Allied forces. He held a telephone conversation with himself ending with the announcement that he was going to climb onto the roof. Then he pushed open the window.

It was ideal. From the bed, he could climb through the window without any trouble. A few minutes later he was in the gutter. It was a little slippery, being coated with wet green slime and dead leaves. But, slippery or not, it was so beautiful up there that it was well worth taking a few steps along the gutter. He could look down on to the roof of the neighbors' house. That was certainly something he could boast about to Joost, his friend from next door. Happily he turned the corner and came face to face with the blank wall of the town hall—how disappointing! He turned about and soon reached the next corner. Now he was on the street side, and that was fun.

Jochem noticed the baker look up and stop his cart. Then Mrs. Van de Ende came running out of her house with her hands in the air. What could be the matter? Perhaps something was happening near their front door? He leaned forward to look over the edge of the gutter—and only then did he become aware of the frightening drop. It was terrible. If he fell, he would almost certainly be killed. And now he realized that all those people were calling to *him.* Jochem was suddenly scared. He crouched down on his knees and clasped the side of the gutter. His lips began to tremble and two minutes later he was crying pitifully.

For a few minutes Mrs. Van Beusekom had forgotten about Jochem. She was worried about Erica and Michiel, sensing that they were up to something about which she knew nothing. As always, her thoughts wandered to her dead husband, who could no longer help her with Jochem's upbringing. The boy really needed a firm hand now. Where was Jochem, anyway? She looked in the sitting room, the garden, and the barn. Then she opened the door to the cellar.

"Jochem!"

No answer. She was on the point of going upstairs to look when someone rang the doorbell. She quickly took off her apron and went to open the door.

"Madam, do you realize that your son is on the roof?"

She ran outside, where a crowd of about twenty people were already gazing upward. Her heart missed a beat or two.

"Jochem, you stay there, I'm coming."

Was she going to have to climb onto the roof? She couldn't even climb a short ladder, and she got dizzy just standing on a chair.

"That gutter is completely rotten," one of the men said. "Nothing has been done about it all during the war, and it wasn't exactly in good condition in 1940. Your foot will go straight through it, I'm sure."

"Mama!" Jochem cried.

"Perhaps we should approach him from the ridge of the roof, over the tiles," someone else said. "Get a few men on the ridge, and then one can be lowered to the little boy on a rope. But how do we get to the ridge?"

"There is an attic window at the back," Mrs. Van Beusekom said hurriedly. "Has anyone got a rope?"

"I've got one at home," the man said. "I'll go and get it."

"That would take too long," someone said suddenly in German. "The boy is beginning to wobble too much. He will fall any minute. Excuse me, ma'am, but could I go through your house, please?" The voice belonged to a German soldier.

"Of course," Jochem's mother whispered, rather surprised. The soldier leaned his bike against the gate and ran into the house. He raced up the stairs, two or three at a time. Less than a minute later, he was struggling out of the attic window. Carefully he lowered himself onto the dangerously sagging gutter.

"Rotten," the soldier muttered. "Old and decayed."

Putting as much of his weight as possible on the tiles, he shuffled along the gutter just as Jochem had done. By the time he reached the front of the house, the street was black with people. Mrs. Van Beusekom, who at first had followed him, had now rejoined the crowd, since Jochem was not visible from the attic window. When he saw the man coming, Jochem had stopped crying. Foot by foot the soldier edged on. Suddenly the crowd screamed in horror as the courageous German's left boot went straight through the gutter. He only managed to save himself by hurling forward so that he lay flat across the gutter. Jochem had been frightened when the strange man fell toward him, but now he felt a strong hand around his left leg. It was a comforting feeling.

"Now we crawl together," the soldier said in broken Dutch. Gently, he pushed Jochem in front of him and they passed around to the other side of the house. The soldier's left knee now hung over the drop as he hooked his foot onto the gutter.

"That whole gutter will collapse any moment," muttered the man in the street who had expressed doubts about its condition a few minutes earlier.

Mrs. Van Beusekom stood there with her hands pressed to her chest, hardly daring to breathe. "Save him, save him," she prayed.

After what seemed like an age, the two reached the back of the house, and Mrs. Van Beusekom went back to the attic. The soldier raised himself cautiously, leaning against the tiles as he pushed Jochem up to the attic window. A minute later, the boy was safely inside, held in the comforting arms of his mother. The soldier, too, was soon safe. Mrs. Van Beusekom grasped his hand gratefully.

"I don't know what to say," she stammered.

The man laughed, pinched Jochem on the cheek, and went quickly downstairs.

"But wait . . ." Mrs. Van Beusekom cried, but he was already out of the front door and on his bike. The

people respectfully made room for him. Someone
yelled "Bravo!" but the praise was blown away in the
wind. The others were too busy recovering from their
fright to say anything. Thirty seconds later, the
soldier had disappeared around the corner of the
street.

———————

"A German?" Michiel asked in utter amazement.
"One of the Boche?"

"A German soldier, one of Hitler's henchmen, an
enemy of our people." Mrs. Van Beusekom was still
pale from the frightening experience; but not
Jochem—he had almost forgotten all about it already.

Michiel went out and looked up. He saw the broken
gutter and realized how high it was. He went inside
again, still shaking his head in disbelief.

"Mother, why did a German have to do it? What
were the other people doing all this time? Were they
just looking? What were you doing yourself?"

"I realized I couldn't do it. You know what a
heroine I am when it comes to climbing! The others
all talked about it, but I don't think they had the
courage either. It was very frightening. Did you see
where he put his foot through the gutter?"

"Yes. Was it very dangerous?"

"It's a miracle that he didn't fall to his death."

Meanwhile, Erica had come in and she too had to
hear the story. Her first reaction was to hug Jochem.
She didn't seem all that surprised to hear that the man

who saved him was a German. It surprised Michiel. He still couldn't accept it.

"But why, *why* did he do it?"

"Well, he must have been a decent man," Erica said.

"A German, a decent man? What's he doing here, then?"

"Michiel," Mrs. Van Beusekom said, "there are eighty million Germans, and whether you like it or not, there are some decent people among them, people who don't like this war any more than we do. We don't like Germans, you don't like them, I don't, and neither does Erica, but we will have to be grateful to this one, whatever else you think. At least, *I* am grateful to him."

"Perhaps he was a member of the firing squad, too," Michiel said stubbornly.

"I can't believe that. And even . . . no, I don't believe it."

"They don't have to be in the firing squad if they don't want to be," Erica said.

Michiel was silent. It was so much easier to hate *all* the Germans. And now he had to admit that this soldier had proved himself to be much more public-spirited than all their neighbors put together. He looked at the fair young head of his little brother. A fall of thirty feet onto the pavement . . .

"All right, just this one," he grunted. "The other seventy million, nine hundred and ninety-nine thousand, nine hundred and ninety-nine are still murderers."

"There are probably a few less," his mother said. "If there's one good one there may well be others. Come on, Jochem, time for bed."

"I won't go on the roof again," Jochem said, "unless that nice man comes with me."

Chapter 11

One Wednesday afternoon, Michiel prepared to visit Jack. He strapped a knapsack onto his bike, containing some sandwiches, two apples, a bottle of milk, a pan of cooked red kidney beans, and a piece of ham. Not a bad haul this time, he thought. He cycled off toward the Dagdaler wood. He did not take the path leading to the newly planted firs immediately, because there was someone cycling behind him. He turned right instead of left and after a few hundred yards he stopped and went back. There was some traffic on the Damakker road, so he cut straight through the forest. As usual, he hid his bike in the bushes and walked the rest of the way. He reached the northeast sector without meeting anyone. There he crouched down on his knees and started his usual slinking journey. In spite of his prowling skill, Jack heard him coming and was waiting for him in the opening to the cave.

"Don't be frightened," he said. "We've got a visitor."

In spite of the warning, Michiel was surprised. It could not be Erica, because she had been at home when he left.

"Who is it?"

"Go and see for yourself."

He went into the cave and saw someone lying on the improvised bed. But only when his eyes had gotten used to the dark did he see who it was.

"Dirk!"

"Hello, Michiel."

Dirk raised himself. He looked hideous. His nose was crooked; one of his eyes was so swollen it could not be seen at all. There was a nasty, raw patch on his left cheek. His mouth was half open—apparently he could not close it.

"Dirk, what have they done to you?"

Dirk tried to smile. It was more of a grimace.

"Fortunately I don't have a mirror."

"Did you escape?"

"Yes, I jumped out of a train. That was the night before last. Did you bring any food? I haven't eaten a thing for two days. Yesterday I hid in a woodshed all day. I almost froze to death. Last night I walked here—or, rather, I stumbled here."

"Thundered would be nearer the mark," Jack said.

"I almost shot him. He came crashing through the trees as though he were a whole infantry battalion."

"I'd almost blacked out," Dirk said.

Michiel quickly opened the knapsack and started giving Dirk something to eat.

"Soft things, please. Those kidney beans look good. And milk, gorgeous. I've hardly any teeth left, you know. Sorry, Jack, I'm afraid I'm eating most of your food. You take the apples, I can't bite those."

"Never mind," Jack said.

"I'll bring some more," Michiel said. "Maybe even today, but certainly by tomorrow."

"Do you think you could bring another blanket?" Jack asked.

"I'll try."

Dirk ate everything he could manage to chew. Then he said, "I eat your food, I lie on your bed, and I'm a nuisance, I know."

"But it's *your* cave," Jack said.

"Michiel's obviously been taking good care of you."

"He has."

"He has even taught you Dutch."

"He's mostly done that by himself, from a book," Michiel said modestly. "And he's probably picked up the rest from a certain girl called Erica."

"Your sister?"

"I'm sorry, but she's always here."

"I'm not sorry at all," said Jack.

"Has the leak come through her, then?"

"What are you talking about? What leak?"

"We were betrayed."

"Erica hasn't betrayed anyone. Anyway, she only joined us later."

"Someone must have betrayed us. The whole thing was one big leak. For instance, why did they go and arrest Bertus Van Gelder? Jack told me about it. Did you show that letter to anyone, Michiel?"

"No, certainly not. I can swear to that. I hid it in one of the chicken coops. But you, Dirk, did you . . .? They beat you so much. . . . Didn't you mention Bertus's name? I was sure . . ." Everyone was silent. Dirk had thrown himself back again. He looked exhausted and he had closed his eyes.

"They beat me up terribly," he said faintly, "but I swear that I didn't divulge a thing." He started breathing heavily through his deformed nose. Jack signaled to Michiel, as if to say, "Better leave him alone now."

"I'll see what I can get together in the way of food and blankets. I'll be back tomorrow at the latest," Michiel whispered. "Can you manage till then?"

Jack nodded. "Don't take any unnecessary risks. We'll manage here."

"All right, see you. Look after him."

"Roger."

Michiel immediately set about collecting as much food as possible. He went to Van Coenen, with whom he was on friendly terms, and bought bacon, eggs, bread, and cheeses. He managed to scrounge a loaf of bread from the baker. He had spent almost all his

money on food, and that would present a problem in
the future. However, he also found two horse rugs in
a large chest in the loft. Unfortunately, it was too late
by this time to go to the forest so he had to wait until
the following morning. The next day he was lucky
because his mother went out with Jochem for an hour.
This gave him the chance to boil the eggs. He even
remembered to take some salt. The only problem was
how to reach the forest unnoticed, with such a bulky
parcel. It would certainly be noticed if he cycled
around with it. He decided to do it in stages. First he
took one blanket, in which he had hidden some of the
food. This he hid near the place where he usually
started crawling. Then he went back home to collect
the rest. As far as he could tell, nobody had shown an
unusual degree of interest in him, so, at about eleven
o'clock he moved forward with enormous effort
among the small fir trees, dragging the two packs
behind him.

Dirk seemed slightly better. He had more color and
his one good eye looked brighter. Much to Michiel's
surprise, the pile of dry leaves had doubled in size.

"How did that happen?" he asked suspiciously.

"Oh, they just blew in here, during a small gale,"
Jack said.

"Oh yes? There wasn't even a breeze over by us."

"Well, if you really want to know, last night I made
my way to that beech woods not far from here and
collected some. I can assure you that no one saw me."

"How was your leg?"

"All right."

"Well done."

"Thanks."

Michiel unpacked and the two young men lavished their praise on him. After that, they refused to speak until their stomachs had been satisfied. As soon as they felt full and contented, Michiel said, "I've got a problem."

"Me too," Dirk said. "At least six of them. What's yours?"

"My money is finished. And although the farmers around here aren't mean, I still have to pay something for what I get from them."

"I can solve that one," said Dirk, after some thought. "Go to my mother. She ought to be told that I'm safe, anyway. Don't go to my father—he would be so scared he'd give the whole game away. Mother must tell him. That way, at least he won't know that you're involved. Just tell my mother that there is nothing wrong with me, but that in the interests of safety I have to remain hidden. Also, tell her that I need a parcel of food every week and that you will ensure that it's delivered. You'll see, she'll manage very well indeed—"

"All right, I'll do that."

For a moment, they didn't know what to say to each other.

"What's the weather like?" asked Dirk at last.

"Not too bad, cloudy."

"That's better than clear. We can certainly do without frost, even though you got us two blankets. Is it going to stay like this?"

"I don't know that much about the weather, and, as
you know, we haven't had a radio for a long time
now."

"Let me take a look." Dirk stood up and walked to
the cave opening. He moved like a cripple, and the
shock of this made Michiel bite his lip.

"Did they do that, too . . .?"

Dirk nodded. "*Now* do you understand why I have
a score to settle with whoever betrayed me? I'll tell
you something. I jumped out of the train at Stroe. Not
far from there, at Garderen, I have an old friend who
would have hidden me. But I came here. I'm determined to find out who the traitor is."

"Schafter," Michiel said.

"Schafter? How do you know? I always thought
that Schafter was . . ."

"Scafter was what?"

"I don't know. Maybe he's on the other side, who
knows? I would never have thought it, though. I
always thought he just pretended to be pro-German. I
don't know why. But I might be wrong."

"You *are* wrong," Michiel said. "I have proof."

"Out with it, then."

"It is quite a long story. You tell yours first, then I
can go on from there."

"O.K.," Dirk said. "Here we go; I'll start at the
beginning:

"At the beginning of the war, in 1941 or thereabouts,
I was working for the Forestry Commission. I got

orders to plant three plots of firs here in the Dagdaler woods. I was only eighteen then and although we weren't really aware of the war over here, I decided, in a romantic mood, that I would dig a hiding place— never guessing that it would one day serve this purpose—right in the middle of a plot of thick firs where no one would ever find it. I told nobody about it. Even later on, when I became a member of the underground movement, I still kept quiet about it.

"It proved really useful when I found Jack with a broken leg and a hole in his shoulder. I took him in a carriage to a doctor who was in hiding nearby. A short time afterward, they picked him up. How he got hold of plaster, I don't know. I think he concocted something himself out of bone, glue, and chalk, or something like that."

"Yes, Erica thought it was a very strange kind of plaster," Michiel said.

"Anyway, Jack was bound up and I dragged him here."

"We knew all that already," Michiel said.

"Listen, I don't know exactly what you do know. So we'll just go through the whole story, shall we?"

"Right," said Michiel.

"I didn't mention Jack to the other members of the underground movement," Dirk continued. "You see, I wasn't quite sure if everyone there was completely trustworthy. For instance, there was one member, maybe he still is a member, a man called Schafter. He used to say that he played up to the Germans a bit, just to fool them. I always believed him—but judging

by what you said just now, Michiel, I'm afraid I've
been too trusting.

"So I didn't say anything about Jack, and if you
think about it, Jack's presence here is about the only
thing that hasn't leaked out. That's something worth
bearing in mind, isn't it?

"Last autumn we got orders from our commander
to raid the distribution office at Lowsand. There were
three of us: myself, Willem Stomp, who's dead now,
and a third man who escaped and whose name I won't
mention. The commander thought three would be
enough. He said that no one else would know anything about it."

"The commander wasn't Postma, by any chance?"

Dirk looked surprised. "How did you know that?"

"Guessed. It doesn't matter. Go on."

"I realized that if anything went wrong, Jack here
would starve. But if I had given the letter myself to
Bertus Van Gelder, who was in the underground too,
then he would have known that I had something to
hide. That's why I gave the letter to you, Michiel. If
everything had gone all right, then Bertus would
never have known anything about it. He probably
doesn't, even now. You always seemed to me to be a
quiet, careful person, and I thought I could trust you."

"You could, even though I have spoiled just about
everything," Michiel said unhappily.

"I believe you, but let me go on. In the distribution
office at Lowsand we walked straight into an ambush.
They were waiting for us. You know what that means,
of course? Someone betrayed us. But who? Who

knew about the plan? The three of us who had to carry it out; Mr. Postma, who said he had told no one else about it; and you, Michiel; that was all."

"Isn't it possible that the third man in your party was allowed to escape because he had betrayed the plan beforehand?"

"I thought of that too, but it seems very unlikely to me. You'll see why in a minute."

"What happened during the raid?"

"Well, that's the whole point. We had agreed that the third man would keep watch, while Willem and I went inside. The Germans had probably counted on the third man remaining close to the door because they had hidden themselves behind a birch hedge that runs alongside the building. But in fact we had decided that our man should walk around the office in a large circle to make sure that no one approached from any direction. So when we reached the door he had already fallen behind as planned. Just as we threw open the door, the Germans appeared. There were at least fifteen guns trained on us. I knew at once that we didn't stand a chance, and raised my hands. But Willem ran straight into the little office, vaulted over the counter, went through the door that leads to the small room at the back, and tried to escape through the window. Unfortunately, he misjudged the Boche badly. Some had been stationed behind the building, too, and they shot him dead immediately. I heard the shots, but at the time I didn't know exactly what had happened. Meanwhile, they pushed me toward a police car. 'Where is the third man?' they snarled.

"I played stupid and said that I didn't understand any German—I'm not very good at it, actually. Later I said that there had only been two of us. 'We've already got the second one,' they sneered, as Willem's body was thrown into the car. I wanted to get up to see if I could do something for him, but they hit me in the face and said that he was stone-dead. Then they kept on about the third man again. Now tell me—how could they be so sure that there were three of us?"

Michiel and Jack had nothing to say to that.

"We were betrayed, I am sure of that. They knew exactly how the raid had been planned. Maybe it was Schafter. Maybe he eavesdropped on the conversation between Postma and ourselves. Maybe he found one of Postma's notes. I am keen to know what you have to say about this, Michiel. I must find out—I must be certain. What I had to endure during my imprisonment was so . . . it was . . . Whoever sent me to that is going to pay for it."

Dirk took a deep breath and then went on with his story.

"They searched for a long time and then gave up. Now if the third man had been the traitor, would they have searched for such a long time? They took me to the barracks and left me there for three days. Then the questioning started."

"Hold on," Michiel said. "Do you mean they didn't question you immediately about Bertus Van Gelder, the underground movement, and so on?"

"No, not till three days later."

"So how did they come to think of arresting Bertus the next day? To be honest, I was convinced that they had tortured you so much that you had named him. Please forgive me for thinking that, but, after all, *you* thought I had shown the letter to someone."

"They started interrogating me after three days. At first, it wasn't too bad. The commander was quite reasonable. Of course, he wanted to know whether there was an underground organization behind the raid. I denied it. I said that Willem and I had made the plan ourselves and carried it out alone. He didn't believe it all, nor was he completely convinced that I was lying. Then he started on about the third man. Again, I denied that there had been anyone else, and it was obvious that he knew I was lying about that. He said it would be better for me if I told them who it was, otherwise he would hand me over to the S.S., who had some nice ways of making people talk.

"They sure did! I was taken to the S.S. at Amersfoort. At first I was left alone for a while. Then the interrogation started. Each time I had to undress completely, because that way they could kick me better with their big boots.

"'The name!' they screamed, and whenever I repeated that there had been only two of us, they beat me to the ground and about three of them kicked me in the stomach and face until I lost consciousness."

"And you still didn't betray the third man?" Michiel asked, his face pale with horror. "Why not? How could you bear it?"

"I don't know that myself," Dirk said. "Each time I

was back lying on my bunk, bruised and writhing with pain, I thought, I can't bear it, next time I'll tell them all I know. But then, when I saw their cruel faces again, I resisted, after all.

"On one occasion they didn't beat me. Instead, the S.S. officer who used to question me was very suave. He started by saying that it would be in my own best interests to tell them the name of the third man, and that nothing would happen to him, except one short year in prison. He was so convincing that I almost believed him. But then I remembered all the things they had done to me and I kept my mouth shut. Then that mean look came over his face again. I thought I was in for another beating, but no. Instead, he quietly asked me to get dressed. Well, he didn't have to say that twice. But just as I started to put my socks on, he told me to leave them for a minute and asked me to put my right foot on the desk, which I did. Then he took out a small cudgel, stroked it fondly, and quietly asked whether there hadn't been a third man, after all. 'No,' I said, 'honestly.' Then he smashed my toes with the cudgel and asked me to put my other foot on the desk."

"The monster," said Michiel, who was now as white as a sheet. Jack was swallowing hard.

"Well," Dirk said. "My clogs were rather small for me, but I had to put them on; and my toes are now completely deformed. The funny thing is that I didn't mind all that much, because after that they left me alone for quite some time. I preferred having broken toes to being questioned every other day, I can tell you.

"A few days ago, we were suddenly moved. We weren't told where we were going, but they put us on a train with separate compartments—you know the sort, each with its own door. There were nine of us in one compartment with one armed S.S. man. I was determined to try to escape if there was the least chance. Most of the others looked as if they knew what interrogation was all about, in which case I thought they would be prepared to risk an escape attempt, too.

"Once the train started moving, I soon realized that we were heading for Apeldoorn and I remembered that the Amersfoort–Apeldoorn train slows down for a while at a bend near Stroe. We were not allowed to speak, so I whispered to the others my suggestion of leaping off the train at that point. I reckoned that the S.S. man wouldn't know any Dutch. He didn't, but he did have ears and he rammed the butt of his gun into my ribs. But the others had already got the message.

"When we got near Stroe, we discovered to our horror that the door was locked."

"But how could you try the door, with the soldier sitting there?" Michiel wanted to know.

"The soldier had already been . . . oh well, forget it for the moment. Two lads from Rotterdam, who had been sitting next to him, had taken care of that.

"Well, the door was locked and that meant big trouble. I don't have to tell you what would have happened to us when we got to Apeldoorn, if they had found us with a dead Kraut. But if you're really in trouble, it's surprising what you can do and one of the men managed to force open the door with the soldier's bayonet. When the train slowed down, we all jumped out, one after the other. One man didn't survive it—he hit his head against a pole."

"Didn't the Germans see you?"

"Oh yes. They shot at us through the windows, but it was rather dark and fortunately the train didn't stop. They didn't hit anyone. Apart from that, our luck wasn't in. All eight of us were sitting together, discussing whether we should stick together or split up, when a German patrol came past. Of course, there are many patrols, but they would have to arrive just at that moment, just at that spot! Well, we heard them coming and dived into a ditch, but they had obviously heard something too, because one of them suddenly shouted, 'Halt! Give the password!'

"He had hardly finished speaking when Kryn, one of the chaps with me, started blasting away. He had been a commando, or a paratrooper, or something like that, and had had the sense to take the machine gun from the Kraut in the train. He shot at least three with the first sweep. The others immediately took cover and returned fire. Except for Kryn, none of us could do a thing, apart from making ourselves as invisible as possible. We had no weapons at all.

"'Run!' Kryn yelled, 'I'll keep them occupied.'

"So we slithered our way along the ditch and escaped, and then it was every man for himself. I could still hear shooting for quite some time afterward. I don't know whether Kryn got out alive, but I wouldn't be surprised if he did. He seemed to be one of those people who wouldn't be scared of the devil—the sort that simply can't be killed.

"What happened after that, I've already told you. I hid for a day in a shed, and the following night just managed to get here."

All this talking had made Dirk tired. He threw himself back into the dead leaves and put his hands behind his head.

"And now you can hardly walk?" Michiel asked.

"Well, I can walk a little, otherwise I would never have made it from Stroe. After the war, maybe I'll find a surgeon who can put my toes right again. My eyes and nose and so on will heal by themselves. Anyway, most of what you see on my face happened when I jumped out of the train. I landed badly. Enough of that. It's in the past now, and not all that important. What I want to know is, who is the traitor in Vlank?"

"I still think it's Schafter," Michiel said.

"You do, eh? Then can you explain why Schafter didn't give away the entire underground movement? After all, he knew everyone who was involved."

Michiel had no answer for that. "Shall I tell my story now?" he asked.

Dirk had closed his eyes.

"Better leave it till tomorrow," Jack said.

Chapter 12

All the rest of that day and evening Michiel couldn't
get Dirk's story out of his mind. Such terrible things
really did happen, then. Michiel often thought of
something his father had once said: "In every war,
dreadful things happen. Don't think that it is only the
Germans who are guilty. The Dutch, the British, the
French, every nation has murdered without mercy
and perpetrated unbelievable tortures in times of war.
That is why, Michiel, you shouldn't allow yourself to
be misled by the romance of war, the romance of
heroic deeds, sacrifice, tension, and adventure. War
means wounds, sadness, torture, prison, hunger,
hardship, and injustice. There is nothing romantic
about it."

Michiel knew that *he* could never have endured what Dirk had suffered. He felt an intense admiration for him and was relieved that Dirk had at last managed to escape from the hands of his torturers. Dirk's mother must be informed as soon as possible, so Michiel kept a constant eye on his neighbors' house. Toward late afternoon, he saw Mr. Knopper go out. He quickly jumped over the hedge and found Dirk's mother near the back door, emptying a bin of rubbish.

"I've got some news for you," he said. "Could I come inside for a moment?"

"News? From Dirk?"

Michiel nodded. They went into the kitchen.

"Is it bad news? How did you come to hear of it?"

"It is good news," Michiel said. "Very good news. But you must promise to keep as quiet as the grave about it; and please don't ask me any questions."

"All right, all right," Mrs. Knopper said.

"Dirk has escaped and he is safe, for the moment at least."

Mrs. Knopper immediately forgot all about her promise. "Where is he? How do you know? Is he in good health? Can I see him? How did he escape? Why didn't he come here?"

"That would be far too dangerous, of course," Michiel said. "He is in fairly good health, that's all I can tell you. He needs food, and would like you to make him a food parcel once a week. I'll see that he gets it."

"Of course I'll do that. Oh, what a relief! I suppose I can tell my husband?"

"You can tell him that Dirk is safe, but don't say that I was the one who told you. Apart from him, nobody else is to know anything about it."

"I'll keep my mouth shut. Just tell me whether he is here in Vlank."

"He is in the church tower of Timbuktu," Michiel said. "'Bye, Mrs. Knopper, and don't forget: don't tell your husband that you heard about it from *me*."

"No, I won't. I will have a food parcel ready tomorrow. Can't you tell me just a little more, Michiel? Can I go and see him?"

"No, you can't. I'm sorry, but it really is safer this way," Michiel said. "Now I must hurry."

"Good day to you, lad, and, Michiel, thanks—I am so happy."

Michiel left, feeling pleased. He felt sure that Dirk's mother would prepare so much food that he wouldn't have to worry about providing for Jack anymore, either.

———

The next day, it was Erica's turn to go to the cave. Michiel had decided to tell her everything; it would have been impossible to keep Dirk's presence a secret from her. So they both went that day; first Michiel with the parcel from Dirk's mother, then Erica, about ten minutes later.

Dirk felt a bit better. He insisted that Michiel should tell his story, which Michiel did in great detail. He explained exactly where Dirk's letter had been at various times. He described the series of misfortunes he had had on the day he tried to visit Bertus, how Schafter had cycled alongside him, how he finally reached Jannechien the next day, and how Schafter had been seen pointing out Driekusmans Lane to the Germans.

Dirk was not convinced. It was just possible that it could all be a coincidence. However, when Michiel told him about the Koppel ferry, the arrest of ferryman Van Dyk, the death of the Baroness, and, in particular, his conversation with Schafter just before it all happened, he began to think that it was all rather suspicious.

"How can we prove it?" Michiel asked.

"It'll be difficult," Dirk said. "But in any case, Michiel, I'd like you to go to the commander" (he said "commander" because there was no need for Erica to know that it was Postma) "and tell him that he must be on his guard with Schafter. Just say that it's a message from White Leghorn and that you got it through a friend."

"Through Uncle Ben, for instance," Michiel said. "He's with the underground too. Is White Leghorn your code name?"

Dirk nodded.

They talked for a while about all sorts of things, and naturally enough the conversation came around to their father's death.

"Why did they take prisoners in the first place?" Dirk wanted to know.

"They found a dead German in the forest, not all that far from here," Michiel said. "His head had been beaten in. Of course, they wanted to know who was responsible. So they imprisoned ten people and said they would hang them from the chestnut trees in the village square if the culprit didn't surrender within twenty-four hours. Of course, he didn't give himself up; he didn't have the guts. They shot five men, and my father was one of them. They didn't hang them, that would have been even worse. Here, what's the matter with you two?"

Dirk and Jack had gone white and stared blankly at Michiel and Erica.

"But surely you knew all about it already?" Erica said.

Neither of the two men said a word. Erica looked from one to the other. Suddenly Dirk threw himself on his bed, cradling his head in his arms, and sobbed like a child. His whole body jerked. Jack sat down in a corner and hid his face in his hands.

"What are you so upset about?" Michiel asked, not knowing what was wrong. But a horrifying thought had come to Erica. She went up to Jack and shook him by the shoulder.

"Did you two . . .?" She pulled his hands from his face. He looked at her despairingly.

"Did you beat that German to death?"

"Yes," Jack whispered.

Erica released her grip and walked out of the cave like a sleepwalker. Even at that moment, Michiel remembered the need for caution. He followed her out and took hold of her.

"Get down, you're taller than the firs."

Erica bent down and crept along on her stomach through the slender trunks. Michiel followed her. They got their bikes and cycled in silence to the village.

"We won't go home," Michiel said, when they reached the main street. "We must find somewhere to talk."

They rode on past their home and without any discussion automatically made for the "wigwam." This was a disused, dilapidated shed near the Veld-weg, where Erica and Michiel used to have a secret cave when they were younger and still played together. They had thought up hundreds of adventures there, some of which had really happened. Nowadays, long intervals elapsed between visits, for Erica was occupied with her own friends and Michiel wanted nothing to do with them.

The brother and sister put their bikes against the barbed wire enclosing the adjacent field and went inside. Erica sat down on a rusty, upturned bucket; Michiel paced back and forth.

"I'll never be able to forgive them," Erica said.

"It was a vile act," Michiel agreed. "They should have known, or at least Dirk should, that something like that would happen if the body was discovered. Still, you can't say that Dirk is a coward. Just think of all he went through, without revealing the name of the third man."

"That still doesn't mean he would have given himself up if he hadn't been in prison when they discovered the body. He should have surrendered straight after he'd done it. In any case, Jack could have given himself up, because he is in the air force. They wouldn't have shot *him* for killing a German soldier—the rules of war don't allow it!''

"No," Michiel said, "but maybe they hadn't thought it out very clearly."

"I don't understand you," Erica snapped. "Only two months ago, you were saying that if you ever found the man who was responsible, you would tear him to pieces. And now you are defending those two."

"Well, what do you suggest? Do you want to hand them over to the Boche?"

"You must be mad."

"They are depending on us. If we don't look after them, we might just as well turn them in."

Erica was deep in thought.

"I'm just as shocked as you are," Michiel said. "I loved Father at least as much as you did, but I also heard Dirk's description yesterday of all he has suffered. Half an hour ago, I thought he was the greatest hero in the world. Dirk may have been stupid, but that doesn't mean that he is cowardly or weak. I've been much more stupid. In some ways I am responsible for the arrest of Bertus Van Gelder and the death of the Baroness."

"The way I see it, there was nothing you could do about that."

"Did you see how desperate Dirk was? He was even crying."

"That's because he's so weak," Erica said. "He just

broke down because he has no resistance left."

"Weak or not, you can see that it has distressed him greatly."

"That also shows that it was his fault."

They were silent for a while.

"They must be very worried about the future, now that we've gone," Erica ventured.

"I'm not going to let that worry me too much," said Michiel, being hard, in his turn. "When Father was taken prisoner *we* were frightened and uncertain."

"It was awful," Erica whispered. "It was terrible. We really shouldn't make anyone else suffer the same . . ."

Michiel looked at her. His sister's kindness was showing through again.

"Suppose we give them the chance to tell us exactly what happened?" he suggested.

"Do you think we should?"

"Yes."

"All right," Erica said. "Shall we go and see them?"

"Just now?"

"Perhaps we should leave them in suspense for just one night?"

"No, better not."

Smiling faintly, she got up and took her brother's hand.

"Oh well, you're the leader of our underground group, I follow you."

They got on their bikes and cycled back to the Dagdaler woods.

Dirk had calmed down. His dark eyes stared

straight ahead, but he had regained his old compo-
sure. There was little to be read from Jack's face.

"We're listening," Michiel said.

"I'll tell my part first," Jack said. "You know that
I'm a pilot. I was flying a Spitfire. My squadron was
temporarily stationed on a small emergency airstrip in
the south of Holland, near Eindhoven. One day I got
orders to fly over the Yssel and shoot any motorized
vehicles I saw. At first, everything went fine. Near
Hattum I saw a German private car. When they
became aware of me, the men fled into the bushes and
it was easy to send the car up in flames. That didn't
require much ammunition and I had enough to go on.

"But over Zwolle the fun really started. I was
spotted and the 'ack-ack' was soon whistling around
my ears. I tried to get away, but the tail of my
machine was hit. I still had a fair amount of height
and I tried to get outside the Occupied Zone, despite
the fact that my direction equipment was no longer
functioning properly. I flew straight south, but had
only just got clear of the antiaircraft guns when my
engine caught fire. I think the petrol tank must have
been hit too, and the escaping petrol set it ablaze. You
can understand that I had to get out of that machine
quickly. I saw a forest just below—no fun for a
parachutist—but what could I do? I had no choice.

"Fortunately, my parachute opened properly. As I
floated down, I said to myself, 'Oh well, it's P.O.W.
camp for you, Jackie my boy!' But when I saw nothing
but tree tops coming up toward me and no sign of a
gap, that thought gradually changed to, 'Better make

that a little white cross in a small Dutch cemetery!' I landed in a large oak tree. My foot stuck in the fork of two branches and the rest of my body went on falling. My leg snapped like a matchstick, and there I hung, head down, dangling by my broken leg. The whole world was upside down. It was no joke.

"Suddenly I realized that there was a German soldier standing near the foot of the oak tree. He had a gun, which he was aiming at me. 'Don't shoot!' I shouted—in English, because I didn't know the Dutch for it then. In any case, Dutch wouldn't have helped. I should have said it in German. Anyway, the bastard did shoot. I felt something hitting my shoulder, and then lost consciousness, I think. I can only remember thinking I was dead. But what happened after that I can't tell you first hand."

Erica and Michiel, who had been listening intently, looked at Dirk, who cleared his throat.

"Yes," he said, "now it's my turn. I was in the forest that day, surveying the areas that had to be thinned. I had my chopping knife with me. I always keep my ears open for odd sounds and suddenly I heard a noise. I thought it might be a deer and I wanted to try to hit it with my knife. I'd been practicing my throwing for some time. First of all, it was just for fun, but later more seriously. Anyway, we could certainly have done with some venison.

"So, as quietly as I could, I crept toward the noise. I had just discovered that it was a German soldier with a girl whom I didn't know when something very unexpected happened. Almost directly above me there was the sound of breaking branches and screaming, which gave all three of us the fright of our lives—the German soldier, the girl, and myself. Obviously, Jack must have screamed when he broke his leg. But really, at first it sounded as though the devil himself were descending on us.

"The girl jumped up and ran away screaming. The soldier jumped up too, and I saw him take out a pistol. He obviously felt threatened. Then I heard someone shout in English, who must have been Jack, 'Don't shoot,' and I realized that the strange figure hanging upside down and half-covered by a parachute must be an Allied Forces pilot who had baled out of a crippled plane. The German started shooting, which made me furious. Perhaps he panicked and didn't know what he was doing, but it's just as likely that he really wanted to kill. Some of our German friends can be like that. Anyway, when he took aim for the second time, I threw my knife at him. I had never thrown so well in my life. I hit him right on the back of the head. If he had been wearing his helmet, nothing would have happened, but he had taken it off while he was courting. The helmet was still lying on the grass. The soldier fell, stone-dead.

"Then I realized that I had landed myself in one almighty mess. On the one hand, there was a badly injuried British pilot, hanging unconscious, upside down, from a tree, whom I had to hide from the Germans. On the other hand, there was the body of a German soldier whom I had killed and for whose murder I would be shot without hesitation if it were discovered. I could also be shot for hiding a pilot. I climbed up the tree, cut a piece of cord from the parachute, and tied it around Jack. Then I wound it around a branch so that I could lower him slowly. Loosening the foot that was stuck was a terrible job. In the first place I could hardly reach it. Secondly, it meant moving his obviously broken leg up and down. Luckily, Jack remained unconscious."

"The pain was so agonizing," Jack interrupted, "that I didn't know or care what was happening."

"But you did manage to convey to me that the body had to be hidden," Dirk said. "I realized that if the body of a murdered Boche was discovered, the village would be in all kinds of trouble. I thought of everything, even giving myself up. I swear it. But it isn't all that easy to walk straight to your death.

"At last I thought I had found the answer. I said to myself, 'Now, if a pilot kills a German, that is a simple act of war.' So I decided to wrap the body in the parachute. Then, if the Germans found it, they would conclude that a plane had crashed in the forest and the soldier had lost a fight with the pilot. I dug a hole in the ground with my knife as well as I could, but there were so many tree roots that I couldn't make it very deep. I put the German, wrapped in the parachute, in it and covered him with a layer of earth. Apart from his pistol, I didn't take anything from him. Jack's got that in his belt."

"I didn't hear anything about a parachute being found around the corpse," Michiel said.

"Perhaps someone found him earlier and had taken

the parachute," Erica suggested. "You know that
everyone wants parachute material."

"That's possible," Michiel admitted.

"And I've already told you how I took Jack to the
doctor in a carriage and how I managed to drag him to
the cave," Dirk said finally. "Several weeks later, I
was taken prisoner myself. Now you know everything. And so do I. I know now that I should have
given myself up after all."

After hearing Dirk's story, they could hardly say
that it had really been anyone's fault. But even so,
something had come between them: between Michiel
and Dirk; and between Erica and Jack. Looking at it
rationally, neither Jack nor Dirk had done anything
wrong—certainly, Jack had not. He had been in too
bad a state to be aware of anything. And Dirk . . .
Dirk really deserved a medal for his determined,
courageous behavior, Michiel thought. Nevertheless,
his father's death had come between them now.
Everything that had seemed beautiful and honorable
and courageous in war had been spoiled. His father
had been right—there was nothing romantic about
war.

In spite of their feelings, he and Erica firmly
declared that they condemned no one. They themselves shouldn't have walked off so hastily. Dirk had
done the right thing. If there were a culprit, then it
was whoever had taken the parachute. But in fact, he
could hardly be called the culprit either, just irrespon-
sible and unthinking. He could at least have told the
Germans that the body had been wrapped in a para-

chute. They begged Dirk to stop reproaching himself. They even made jokes about Jack, hiding in trees to spy on courting couples. And yet . . .

"It will have to wear off," Erica said. "I will get used to the idea. After all, Jack has remained the same. He didn't do anything wrong." So she and Michiel continued to find food and to care for their two friends.

But feeding rabbits would be less trouble, Michiel thought to himself.

Chapter 13

Even in times of darkness, hunger, and danger, the clock still moves. January passed. February passed. The stream of hungry people from the west became larger and slower. They were weak and thin. The strongest, the young men, had either been dragged off to Germany or had gone into hiding. No new Mayor was appointed. Mrs. Van Beusekom still lived in the Mayor's house with her children. Every night, hollow-eyed, stumbling, exhausted people streamed into the house. Michiel was still pondering on the betrayal. He had gone over everything in his mind a thousand times. A thousand times he came back to Schafter—and he was still not absolutely certain.

One Sunday afternoon, after his sixteenth birthday,

he went for a walk with Uncle Ben. They walked through the fields where the winter rye was looking strong and green already. They went on through the meadows where the year-old calves seemed unperturbed by the March winds.

"The buds are getting bigger," said Uncle Ben, as he broke a twig from an elder bush. "Spring is almost here. It's about time. The people in the big towns have suffered from severe cold this winter. There is no coal left; many trees in the parks have been felled; wooden sheds have been demolished. People have done all they can to provide a little fuel for their stoves, to warm their frozen bones, and cook their tulip-bulb soup."

"Soup from tulip bulbs?"

"Oh yes, tulips have become a delicacy. Do you remember the story about the siege of Leiden, in 1574? The people were eating dogs, cats, rats, and even almost their Mayor, then. It hasn't quite got that far yet, but it won't be long."

"Hm," Michiel murmured. The fact that people were hungry was nothing new to him. Few people had occupied themselves as much as he had with the army of hungry people that passed by every day.

"When do you think the war will be over?" he asked.

Uncle Ben shrugged his shoulders.

"I know a clairvoyant who has predicted the date of Hitler's capitulation four times now. Every time, her dates are proved wrong by events."

"Everyone says that it can't be long now. The Allies

are heading straight for Berlin and they say that the
Russians are doing the same."

"I wouldn't shout too soon," Uncle Ben said. "Ever
heard of the Ardennes offensive?"

"No, what was that?"

"On the sixteenth of last December the German
troops, supported by a division of tanks, started a very
strong offensive in Belgium near the Ardennes under
the command of General Von Manteuffel. The Allies
were scared stiff. They hadn't realized that the Boche
were still so strong. Fortunately it failed, because the
Germans couldn't take Bastogne. Otherwise, I'm not
sure what would have happened. And don't forget the
secret weapons, the V1's and V2's. There are more of
those nasty missiles descending on London every
day. People are also whispering about a terrible new
bomb. Apparently, if one is ever manufactured, its
effects will be horrifying. They say that just one of
those bombs could devastate a whole town."

"Don't the Americans have any secret weapons?"

"I don't know, I hope so."

They were silent for a while. According to Uncle
Ben, then, the war might still last for quite a while.
Michiel thought, Long enough for Schafter or some-
one else to organize a few more dirty tricks.

I wish, he thought aloud, that I knew how to find
out whether or not someone is a traitor.

"A traitor? Who?"

"Someone in the village."

"Whom did he betray?"

"Doesn't matter," Michiel said.

"I had a problem like that once," Uncle Ben said.

"Oh yes? What did you do?"

"The man was in the same underground movement as I was, but I didn't trust him. So I left a note, seemingly by accident, in a place where I knew he would find it. On the note I had written that a certain family was hiding Jews. And the next day the house was raided."

"And the Jews?"

"There weren't any, of course. I had chosen a family whom I knew to be pro-German. But I had got the information I wanted."

"What did you do then?"

"That doesn't matter." Now it was Uncle Ben who was being secretive, and he smiled knowingly.

Michiel liked the idea. He should be able to do something similar with Schafter. But how could he get a letter to Schafter? He could just throw it into the letter box. If he waited until Schafter left his house, then he could do it without being noticed. Schafter lived by himself, so that was no problem.

But what should he put in the letter? "Dear Mr. Schafter, I hereby inform you that Mrs. X is hiding Jews, yours sincerely, Michiel Van Beusekom." No, that was nonsense.

What then? Well, for a start, he must not sign it; make it an anonymous note. If Schafter didn't react, then it would not matter. But on whom could he cast suspicion in the letter? He didn't know of anybody who was pro-German, except Schafter himself.

"How do you know for certain that someone is pro-German?"

"Well," Uncle Ben said, "that's difficult. Didn't I hear you say once that a certain Schafter was suspect?"

"Yes," Michiel said, "but I'm not sure," not revealing his real thoughts. "Just imagine if he *were* hiding Jews, I would never forgive myself."

"Well," Uncle Ben said, and then thought for a moment. "It doesn't have to be Jews. You might think of something else. For example, that there are weapons hidden in the Green Cross building, near your home. It's empty, isn't it? Let them have a raid there."

Michiel had never thought his uncle a fool, but now he began to think that he was walking beside a genius.

"Marvelous," he said. "I'll send the suspect an anonymous letter and then we'll see what happens."

Uncle Ben threw him a sideways glance.

"Look, my young friend," he said, "I don't want to poke my nose into your affairs, but aren't you poking your nose into affairs that are rather beyond your years?"

"I'm not young anymore," Michiel said indignantly. "I am sixteen."

"I'm amazed, old man," Uncle Ben said. "What an age! You are graying at the temples already, or is it just soft baby hair?"

That remark made Michiel kick a tree trunk so hard that his uncle, who was standing right under it, got soaked by a shower of raindrops.

Michiel set to work as soon as he reached home. After several attempts, he wrote, in large printed letters:

> **The occupier might like to know there is an arms cache in the Green Cross building.—W.**

That "W." was just to give it more authenticity. It didn't mean anything. He wanted to show the letter to Uncle Ben, but didn't, thinking, the less others knew about your business, the safer it is.

The next morning, Michiel walked to Schafter's house. He had intended to hide behind some bushes about a hundred yards from the house, but he was lucky. As he passed the grocer's, he saw Schafter in the shop. That made it easy. He had to hurry now, to complete his mission before Schafter returned from his shopping. Arriving at Schafter's house, he looked quickly around him, and saw only the ever-present stream of travelers on the road. Briskly, he opened the gate. Ten seconds later, the note was in the letter box. Even if a neighbor had noticed, it wouldn't matter. Nobody talked to Schafter. The man was avoided as though he had an infectious disease.

After that, there was nothing to do but wait. For the first twenty-four hours, Michiel could hardly stop from looking at the Green Cross building. When he was at home he was constantly walking to the window to see if anything was happening. But nothing did. The building just stood there, lonely and unvisited. It stayed like that for a whole week. No German even looked at it.

Now I still don't know anything, he thought. Either Schafter isn't a traitor, or else he has recognized it as a trap, and isn't going to bite. Uncle Ben dropped in one day, and asked what had happened to Michiel's little plan.

"Failed," the young plotter said, and that was all.

Another week passed, in which nothing special happened, apart from the usual misery of the travelers and an abortive bombardment of the barracks (all the bombs had landed in a field). And then, fifteen days after Michiel had put the note in Schafter's letter box, it happened. One afternoon they came. A military car stopped in front of the building and five soldiers got out. They forced the door open and went in. Michiel saw it all from the living room.

"Whatever are you looking at?" his mother asked.

"A raid on the Green Cross building."

His mother came to the window too.

"Whatever are they doing there? That building has been empty for the last three years."

"I haven't a clue." He said it so triumphantly that his mother gave him a quick glance.

The soldiers stayed for half an hour. Then they got into the car again and drove off. The door remained ajar.

"Tomorrow I will go to Dirk," Michiel thought. He

hadn't told his friend anything about the trap. He didn't want to do that before he was sure it had succeeded. Now he was certain. There could no longer be any doubt that Schafter was a dirty traitor. Dirk could work out for himself how to settle his debt with the man.

———————

There was an aid committee in Vlank, which had been set up by a few thoughtful women who tried to help the most needy cases among the travelers. If someone collapsed and could not get up again, he was taken to the small emergency hospital, which had six beds. Then, for a few days, he would be looked after with care and sympathy. Most of the work was done by Erica. She joined only after the committee had been in existence for some time. Because she had plenty of time, was young and strong, and as she knew something about nursing, she soon became one of the pillars of the Ladies' Committee. Also, during the winter, she had been able to steal the dressings for Jack, which had come in very handy indeed.

The Ladies' Committee had also done something else—it had fitted out the village hall to serve as a kind of hostel. There was some hay on the floor and anyone who could not find shelter for the night could sleep there. Every evening, from seven until one minute to eight, Erica was in that hall. Helped by a few first-aid people, she pricked blisters, dressed sore spots, and put plaster on open wounds. Michiel often went to collect her. This had two advantages: first of all, the pinchcat could stay at home longer, and secondly, Erica didn't have to walk home by herself.

Later, when Michiel thought back over the war, he often remembered that hall with the first-aid people dressing wounds by the light of one candle, and the murmur of voices in the darkness. It had a very special atmosphere. The feeling of misery and sadness contrasted with the feeling of comfort.

The only lighted area was around the small platform on which Erica worked. Otherwise, the place was in darkness. You could tell only from the rustling of the hay that there were people there.

Usually the minister came in just before eight o'clock. He would walk down the gangway toward the light, treading carefully to avoid stepping on the outstretched hands. Bending over the light, a mere arm's length from the sores and blisters, he would read a few sentences from a pocket Bible. Then he would say a few words to his invisible audience. "Dear people, I can't see you, but I know, I feel, that you are there. How we need each other in times like these."

Michiel often went a little early, to listen to the minister. He hardly ever went to church, but in that tiny hall it was different. There, the minister didn't speak over the heads of the people, but straight to them. Strangely, it was just as if the breathing and rustling of these people was their way of responding to him.

Each time, Michiel was surprised that no one called out from the dark shadows, "Go away, with your religious nonsense." Nobody said, "I am a Catholic or a Methodist, and I don't want to hear a Reformed minister." Quite the opposite. They held on to the hem of his coat and said, "Thanks, minister, how kind of you to come." Once there was a man who asked for a page from the Bible, just any page. He said, "I have never believed in anything, but now I need to have something from God."

Michiel could not understand it, but he always had the feeling that the people in the village hall were content. Why was that? Was it because they were tired from the long journey and were glad to rest their exhausted bodies on the hay? Was it because they were all having a difficult time? They were still hungry; they were far from home. The next day they would have to drag themselves on again. They would have to hide once more from the planes and wonder where they would find shelter during the night. It was very strange. His father had been right when he said the war meant tears, hunger, hard times, fear, and pain, and yet . . . In that hall, Michiel sensed that there was also something to be learned from war; something that he would be able to use all his life.

———

That evening, after the raid on the Green Cross building, Michiel was about to go and collect Erica when somebody rang the doorbell. He opened the door, expecting yet another guest, but there stood Schafter.

"Hello . . . hello, Mr. Schafter, come in," he stammered.

"No," Schafter said.

"What can I do for you?"

"See here," Schafter said. "You put a note in my letter box. I don't know why you did it, but I don't like it. This afternoon there was a raid on the Green Cross building. They say that nothing was found there."

"Where did you get the idea that I put a note in your letter box?"

"I know."

"How do you know?"

"That's none of your business. No doubt you suspect that I'm a traitor. I don't suspect *you* of being one, and that's why I'm not surprised that no arms were found in the building. I want to tell you that I have never betrayed anything to the Germans."

"But—but that raid on the Green Cross building, why did that take place, then?"

"That's exactly the point," Schafter said. "You start jumping to conclusions—wrong conclusions. I don't know why the building was raided. But I do know something else: I threw your silly note into the stove and told no one about its contents. No one! You understand?"

"No . . . er, yes," Michiel stammered.

"Good evening."

Schafter turned around, with an angry shrug of his shoulders, and disappeared into the night.

Instead of collecting Erica, Michiel went to his room in the attic to think. He sat for some time on the edge of his bed, staring into the darkness. Once again, he felt uncertain and confused. How did Schafter know that he had put the note in his letter box? No one knew that, not even Uncle Ben. Michiel was sure he had seen Schafter in the grocer's shop. The neighbors? Maybe a passerby had recognized him? But he had looked around and he hadn't seen anybody. He might have been wrong, but that wasn't very likely; no one talked to Schafter anymore. Neither was it likely that Schafter had taken the letter around to everyone in the neighborhood, asking if anyone had seen who had put it in his letter box. It wasn't that sort of note.

Was he that stupid? Everything he did went wrong. He was always letting somebody down. Didn't everyone say that he was as close-mouthed as an oyster? Hadn't his father and mother told him that he knew how to keep a secret before he was four years old? Hadn't Erica told him all his life that he never told her anything? And yet, everything he did seemed to be very clear, open, and obvious to everyone?—well, to Schafter, at least? Did the man have two faces, or was he clairvoyant?

His trap had failed, that much was clear to him. As long as there were so many doubts remaining, he could not tell Dirk for certain Schafter was the traitor. In a subdued mood, he went downstairs.

"Who was that at the door?" his mother asked.

"Father Christmas," Michiel replied angrily.

"Really, Michiel . . . !"

"I'm sorry, Mother. It was someone looking for shelter. I sent him to the village hall."

How easily he lied nowadays. It was no trouble at all.

"Aren't you going to collect Erica?" his mother asked. "She hasn't got the pinchcat."

Michiel looked at his watch. It was two minutes to eight—he could just make it. He ran out, violently pressing the button on the pinchcat, as though it was all its fault.

Chapter 14

Ten days passed. It was the first of April. Nobody produced a good April Fool's joke. April 2nd, April 3rd . . . The rumors of the Allied advance became more optimistic every day. When would Hitler give in? The war was drawing to a close, that was certain.

For Michiel and Erica, that was reason enough to talk Jack out of his idea of trying to rejoin his squadron. Jack was restless. He felt fit, and spring was coursing through his veins. It had not been much fun, living in an underground cave all winter.

"I want to get back to the action," he said. "I'm sure they can't manage without me."

"Why take unnecessary risks? Everyone's saying the war is nearly over," Michiel argued.

"You stay with us. I want to celebrate the liberation with you, and I also want to introduce you to my mother," Erica said.

But Jack wanted to get away. He was always fidgeting, and had begun to get careless as well. One day, as Michiel lay waiting in the undergrowth on the edge of the fir-tree plantation, he nearly had a heart attack when he heard a voice whisper, "Hands up!" He turned to stare down the barrel of a revolver.

"Ha, ha!" laughed Jack.

Michiel was furious—"It's not funny. We aren't a couple of Boy Scouts playing at soldiers on an army camp in England. Twelve people were shot at Hardewijk yesterday. The war isn't over yet—on the contrary, the Boche seem to be enjoying it more every day, judging by the numbers of captives and political prisoners they're shooting."

"Sorry," Jack said, guiltily.

But Michiel realized from this little incident that it would be better if Jack could leave. He talked it over with Erica. At first she did not agree, but when he pressed her, and said that Jack might get too reckless being cooped up in the cave, she changed her mind.

"But how?" she asked. "How are we going to get him across the river? How do we get him near the river in the first place?"

"Uncle Ben," said Michiel.

"Uncle Ben?"

"He's in the resistance. He once told me that his

particular work was helping English pilots to get away—and Canadian and American ones as well, of course. Well, he used to do it in the days when they had to go via Spain or by boat across the Channel. I'm taking it for granted that he could get Jack to the south of the country."

"Have you ever told him about Jack?"

"No, not till now. But now I will, and I'll do it as soon as he turns up again."

"Well, all right," Erica said, resigned. "But I would like to have kept Jack here till the war's over."

When Uncle Ben arrived a week later, Michiel asked him straightaway. Uncle Ben frowned.

"Young man, do you mean that you have been hiding an English pilot?"

"Yes."

"For how long?"

"For more than six months."

"How did you find him?"

"I don't think it's necessary for you to know that," Michiel said.

Uncle Ben frowned even more.

"My dear boy, do you know what you are asking? You are asking me to help you smuggle a pilot out of the country. If I am caught, they'll shoot me. That gives me the right to know whether this really is a pilot, or just a German in disguise. It gives me the right to know where he comes from, when he baled out, who has taken care of him up till now, whom he knows, and so forth."

"Yes, I suppose so," Michiel said hesitantly. He

was now so used to the habit of silence, of saying nothing that was not strictly necessary, that it went against the grain to break it. But he realized that Uncle Ben was right. Reluctantly, he told him the story of Jack and Dirk. However, he did not mention the fact that Dirk had killed the German. He told him how Dirk had taken care of the pilot and had hidden him carefully; and he told about the letter and Dirk's imprisonment. Also about the part played in it by Erica and himself.

Uncle Ben laid a hand on his shoulder and said, "That was a man's job. I am proud of you."

Michiel blushed. Until now, he had thought only about his own mistakes. It had never crossed his mind that he might deserve praise.

"Where is the hideout?" Uncle Ben asked.

"It will be better if I tell you that when you have organized the escape. If you are caught, the less you know the better."

"You are much older than your years, my boy," he said. "Most people are talkers. They simply must talk about everything they do or think. It's a kind of assertiveness, I think. Strong characters don't need that sort of thing. They don't need praise or criticism. I'll work out a plan immediately. You must help me, though. How is your pilot dressed?"

"He is wearing the remains of his uniform and an old jacket—rags, really."

"He must have an unobtrusive suit. Can you get that for him? Have a look in your father's wardrobe."

Michiel nodded.

"I have a camera in my suitcase," Uncle Ben went on. "Can you take a snapshot? I'll explain how the camera works. I must have a photo for a false identification card."

Uncle Ben fetched his camera and explained carefully to Michiel how it worked. He made him repeat two or three times what he had to do, until he was convinced that Michiel understood.

"Can you return the camera to me by tomorrow afternoon?"

"I think so."

"Fine. I don't have to tell you that your pilot must wear ordinary clothes when you take his photo, do I?"

"Hm," Michiel said, "good thing you told me."

Uncle Ben muttered, "Well, that makes—photo on Wednesday, developed on Thursday, false identification card organized over the weekend. By that time, I can arrange the escape route. Right, that makes it Monday. On Monday I will take him to the contact address from where he will be sent on."

"Monday? As soon as that?"

"Yes, I think so."

Michiel set to work immediately. Most of his father's clothes were much too big for Jack, who was very thin. But he found a sports jacket that looked smaller than the other clothes and a pair of trousers that could be drawn together with a belt. These would have to do, he thought. Many people had lost weight during the war, after all. While he was getting the things out of the cupboard, his mother saw him. She stopped in the door and saw the clothes spread out on the bed. She started to say, "What are you . . . " then apparently thought better of it, turned around, and very quietly shut the door. Michiel suddenly realized that he had inherited his mother's character. She could hold her tongue too; but in addition she managed not to ask questions, and that was much more difficult.

The photo was taken without a hitch. Jack was delighted when he heard that he was to leave the hideout on Monday. Moreover, he was excited by the sense of danger. Dirk was a bit jealous. He was quite strong now, and would have liked some action as well, but he could not walk well enough. If he reported to the resistance movement he would only be a burden to them.

"This uncle of yours, does he know his job?" he asked Michiel. "Has he done this kind of thing before?"

"He's been doing it for years," Michiel said. "If anybody can do it, he can."

Michiel had decided that Erica should take their uncle to the hideout the following Monday. The ties between his sister and Jack were special. It had cost him something to make this decision, but when he saw Erica's sad face, on hearing that the day of Jack's departure was fixed, he felt he must let her do it. He himself had said good-bye to Jack on Sunday.

"I'll come back and see you directly after the liberation. And thanks for saving my life," Jack had said.

"Oh, come off it."

"I mean it. Without Dirk, you, and Erica, I wouldn't have lived through this war. There's a nice thought for you. Later on, when I'm Prime Minister, you two can say, 'But for us Britain would have no government.'"

"Good-bye, Jack. Do exactly as my uncle says."

They shook hands. Michiel's blue eyes met Jack's gray ones.

———

Now it was Monday. Uncle Ben and Erica had just left on foot. They would walk to the fir trees and meet Jack there. Erica had only to show Uncle Ben the way, take her leave, and then go off in another direction. Uncle Ben and Jack would walk to the village, mingling with midday travelers on the road, in order to avoid suspicion. Then they would leave for the south. If they encountered a checkpoint, Jack would show his identification card and stutter. Uncle Ben would explain that he had a speech defect. It should work all right—it simply had to.

Michiel went to cut some wood behind the barn. From time to time, he looked at the church clock. The

minutes ticked by, but so slowly. Uncle Ben and Erica
should be at the fir wood by now. Oh no, it was too
soon. The April sun shone warm on his neck. He put
the axe on the ground and sat down on the chopping
block, his back against the barn. The weariness of a
winter full of strain and hard work crept over him. He
felt a flood of relief at being free of the responsibility
for Jack, and yet he would miss him in a way. He shut
his eyes and turned his face toward the sun. It was
pleasant and warm. He dozed off. Suddenly, he
started awake at the sound of little Jochem's voice. It
sounded very near, as if he were speaking into
Michiel's ear. It took him a moment to realize where
the voice was coming from. It came from the barn.
One of the planks he was leaning on was a little loose
and there was a space between it and the next one.
You did not notice it at first because the planks were
overlapped. Jochem was talking to his mother, and
Michiel could hear every word.

"I've already looked here," Jochem complained. "It
isn't there."

"Were you playing in here?" his mother asked.

"Yes, but only for a little while."

"Have you been to Joost's house?" Joost lived next
door.

"I don't know. Yesterday, maybe."

"Well, your coat may be there. Let's go and ask."

The voices died away. Michiel still felt drowsy from
his sleep, but suddenly his whole body went rigid, as
if he had had a stroke. His eyes grew wider and wider.

That sound . . . voices through the wall . . . The truth struck him, quite clear and distinct. He suddenly knew for certain.

He bit his lips, to overcome the drained feeling in his body. Then he jumped up and ran for his bike. If he could only get there in time . . . ! His clattering tires raced over the road. He just avoided an old lady pushing a doll's buggy, squeezed past Farmer Van Coenen's dung cart, and sped along the Damakker road. There was no time to be careful, no time to look around to make sure nobody saw him. He reached the Dagdaler woods. His brain worked out a plan: clearly, as if it were a film, he knew exactly what to do. At full speed, he took the turn to the left and nearly knocked over Jack and Uncle Ben.

"Michiel, what is the matter?" Uncle Ben cried in alarm. Michiel jumped off his bike and grabbed Jack by the arm.

"Jack, have you got your pistol?"

"Yes, why?"

"Give it to me!"

Taken aback, Jack produced the revolver from under his coat. Michiel grabbed it from his hand, flipped off the safety catch, as Jack had taught him, and pointed the weapon at Uncle Ben.

"Get your hands up!" he shouted.

"What's all this?" Uncle Ben said, and Jack gasped in astonishment.

"This is the traitor," Michiel panted. "He has betrayed Dirk and the Baroness and Bertus, and he was going to walk straight into the German barracks with you, Jack."

"You must be mad," Uncle Ben said.

"I was mad, but I'm not anymore."

"Let's go back to the hideout," said Jack. "It's not very safe here now. Give me the pistol. I was the crack shot of my company."

"If you promise to keep him under control."

"You bet."

Jack gave Uncle Ben a shove in the back and nodded in the direction of the hideout. Fortunately, there was nobody in the woods at that time.

"Look here!" Uncle Ben protested. "I really must object to being treated like this. Michiel is talking nonsense. I have been in the resistance for four years."

"That could well be," Michiel sneered. "For four years, a snake in your own nest. That must have meant a lot of victims."

"Don't believe him," Uncle Ben said to Jack. But Jack just made him walk faster.

"If I trust one person in this whole world, it is Michiel," Jack said. "Now, get a move on."

On being made to crawl on his stomach through the trees, Uncle Ben doubled his protests, but to no avail. Dirk was astonished to see them back at the dugout so soon.

"We seem to have your traitor here," Jack said. "He's completely at your disposal." He passed the pistol to Dirk.

"I've never seen this man before," Uncle Ben said.

"And I don't know him," said Dirk.

"He's your traitor, all the same," Michiel grunted.

"You're talking nonsense," said Uncle Ben.

"Why don't we search his pockets?" Michiel suggested.

"Good idea."

Uncle Ben protested vigorously, but the three young men took no notice. The evidence came out bit by bit: a card that gave the owner the right to drive German military vehicles; a list of the German authorities' telephone numbers; a letter from a German girlfriend in Hanover; finally, and most incriminating of all, a letter from the S.S., in which the honorable Mr. Van Hierden was invited to hand over the English pilot to the barracks at Vlank.

"Is his name Van Hierden?" Jack asked with interest.

"Ben Van Hierden, my so-called uncle. For many years, a good friend of my parents. I'll never call him 'Uncle' again, as long as I live!"

"The question is, how much longer is *he* going to live?" Dirk said menacingly.

Ben wiped the sweat off his forehead with the back of his hand.

"You can't prove anything," he stammered.

"Oh no?" Dirk said. "Is none of this stuff proof? Tell me, how did you discover it, Michiel?"

Michiel had great difficulty in telling a coherent story. The wild race on his bike, the excitement, but most of all his anger over his "uncle's" treason, and annoyance with himself for having been fooled, made his head swirl.

"The desperate-chips," he began.

He tried to gather his thoughts.

"I thought I knew quite a bit of Dutch," said Jack, "but that sounded like 'desperate-chips,' whatever they may be."

"Well, I was cutting wood behind the barn," Michiel started again, "where we have a chopping block and some large pieces of wood. Suddenly I heard voices, quite clearly, but without seeing anyone. Apparently my mother and Jochem were in the barn. I noticed a crack between the planks, which explained why I could hear them so clearly. Suddenly I remembered the morning that Dirk gave me the letter. We were in the barn. That same morning Van Hierden had used all the dry bits of wood that my mother keeps for when the stove goes out, the so-called 'chips-for-desperate-moments.' I told him to go and chop some new ones. I remember now that I saw him with the axe. He must have been sitting on the chopping block, as I was this morning, and he would have overheard everything Dirk said.

"Let's recall exactly what he did say. First of all, Dirk told me about the raid on the distribution office at Lowsand. Dirk and his friends fell into a trap and the Boche knew there was supposed to be a third man. Secondly, Dirk mentioned the name of Bertus Van Gelder. He told me to take the letter there if anything went wrong. Van Hierden heard the name, but he also wanted to have the letter. He did not know I had put it in the chicken coop."

Involuntarily, Van Hierden clicked his fingers.

"You had not thought of that, eh?" Michiel sneered, and he continued. "In the evening he searched my room. I caught him, but he said, oh so plausibly, that he was looking for my English dictionary. He wanted to know the word 'dynamite.' He might have looked for the word 'traitor.'"

"I wish you would stop playing with that pistol all the time," Ben Van Hierden said. "They do sometimes go off, you know."

"Well, that would solve some problems; but you are right, I want to have my hands free, so we'll tie you up instead."

Five minutes later, Van Hierden's hands were tied behind his back and his ankles and knees firmly bound with rope. Then Michiel went on with his story.

"When he couldn't find the letter, I suppose he must have reasoned something like this: 'We will leave the raid on Bertus's house until the evening. Then we will find the letter there.' He assumed that I would take it there straightaway. Don't you want to know why I didn't do that?"

Van Hierden did not answer.

"I had nothing but bad luck that day," Michiel continued. "I told you that Schafter came with me to Alderman Kleiweg and that he saw me again later on.

But he could not have known about Bertus. So that was just coincidence, as you said, Dirk. You were right."

"But he pointed out Driekusmans Lane to the Germans," Dirk said, unconvinced.

"Perhaps they just asked him the way, and he told them. He may be a friend of the Germans— everybody says so—but he could not have betrayed Bertus, because he knew nothing about it. But Ben did. And then there's the question of the Koppel ferry. The evening after I helped those people from Rotterdam over the river, he turned up. He hadn't heard about my father's death. He seemed so upset, that to cheer him up I . . . "

"I *was* upset about your father," said Ben Van Hierden. "I always liked your father."

"You could have told the Boche that. It might have made all the difference."

"That was why I was so upset. I had forgotten to tell the commander of the barracks to keep his hands off the Mayor."

"And the secretary, and the minister and all the others? They did not matter, eh?" Michiel said brusquely. "They could be killed. That did not matter. The secretary's wife is now in a psychiatric hospital. She may never get out of it. Did you know that?"

Ben Van Hierden was silent.

"So then, to cheer him up, I was stupid enough to tell him how the Germans were being deceived by the Baroness. You both know what happened. . . . The next morning the whole thing was wound up. And I suspected Schafter. How foolish of me!"

For a while everybody was absorbed in his own thoughts. "I took care that *you* did not get involved," Van Hierden said.

"That should have warned me," Michiel replied. "A couple of times I was sure they were after me. Why didn't you mention my name?"

"Well, I always liked you."

"Watch it, Michiel," Dirk said. "He's going to try to play on your sympathy."

"Why did you do it?" Michiel asked. "Did the Germans pay you?"

"No," Van Hierden answered, and then a fanatical light came into his eyes. "I did it because Hitler is a great man. He understands that some races are meant to be rulers and others slaves. The French, the Italians, and the Spaniards, they're weak. The Jews are just inferior—it would be better if they were all killed off."

Michiel at once thought of the fine, intelligent face of Mr. Kleerkoper.

"The English might be worth something, if they were not so decadent," Van Hierden continued.

"Thank you very much," said Jack.

"But the greatest people of all are the *Herrenvolk*, the Germans. They are tall and blond. They have the best technical and scientific people. They have the greatest composers. They are the best military people. They have discipline and . . . "

"Shut up!" Dirk shouted. "I don't want to hear such driveling rubbish." He rubbed the scar that ran from his left ear to his nose.

"What are we going to do with him?" Jack asked.

"That's what I've been wondering," said Dirk.

"There's only one answer," Jack said.

Dirk nodded.

"Michiel, you can't let them do it," Ben Van Hierden gasped.

"Do what?"

"You can't . . ."

"Is it agreed that we shoot him, then?" asked Michiel grimly.

Dirk shrugged his shoulders. "What else can we do?"

Everybody was silent.

After a while Jack said to Dirk, "You must do it. You suffered most because of him."

"Me? No, please, you do it. You are the military man."

"No," Jack said, "that was not part of my training."

"Couldn't we hand him over to the resistance movement?" Michiel suggested. "And let Mr. Postma decide what to do with him."

Dirk gave this suggestion some thought. "How do we get him to the resistance people? How do we convince them that he is a traitor? Wouldn't we be running an extra risk by letting other people into our secret?"

They could not decide. Jack thought Erica should be asked, too.

At last they decided to leave it till the following day. Van Hierden would have to stay there, even though the hideout was rather small for the three of them.

"Oh, what does it matter?" Jack remarked. "There's not much room in a cockpit either. And where would I be now, but for Michiel racing up so fast on his bike? We can put up with being cramped, just for one night."

"Until tomorrow, then," Michiel said. "I'll let Erica know."

He crawled through the fir wood, found his bike, and went home. After all the uncertainty about the identity of the traitor, he felt relieved that at least some of the riddle was solved. Now he understood how Ben had expedited a letter to Jack's mother so quickly. He must have told the Germans to get the Red Cross to cable the telegram immediately, so that Michiel would be impressed. And it had worked . . . As a result of the quick exchange of letters, he had trusted Ben more than ever. There was only one question left, and that concerned the Green Cross building. How had Schafter known that Michiel had written the note? He shook his head. He still could not understand it.

Chapter 15

The next day they were all together in the hideout again, including Erica. She had been deeply shocked to learn that Uncle Ben was a traitor. Now, in the hideout, she avoided looking at him.

Dirk had thought everything out, and decided what they should do.

"We must hand him over to Mr. Postma," he said. "It may be that he has information that could be important for the resistance. Mr. Postma must try to get that out of him. Hopefully, the war will soon be over, and then the authorities can deal with him and decide his fate. I'm looking forward to being a witness at the trial."

Dirk had probably decided on this course because he could not face carrying out the sentence himself; neither could Jack. It was out of the question for Michiel and Erica to kill him.

"O.K.?" Dirk asked.

He looked around the circle of people. They all nodded in agreement.

"How are we going to get him away from here?" Michiel asked.

"I suggest you take a note from me to Mr. Postma," Dirk replied. "Let's hope Postma knows somewhere to hide our prisoner. You must ask him if he is prepared to come to the edge of the Dagdaler woods to take him off our hands. I will take him at gunpoint from here to the edge of the woods."

"Impossible," said Jack. "Your hands are trembling too much. I'll do it."

But Dirk was adamant.

"Mr. Postma must not meet you, and I don't want him to know where this hideout is. It's not that I don't trust him, but the fewer people who know about this place the better."

"I'll do it, then," Michiel volunteered.

"Do you think you could?"

"Of course, why not?"

"All right, that's settled then."

"If the Germans catch me and find me with a note to Postma, I am lost," Michiel remarked. "Wouldn't it be better if I went without a note?"

"Mr. Postma might not believe you. I'll try to write

in such a manner that nobody will understand what it's about."

They all agreed on the plan and Dirk wrote the following note:

M.V.B. can be trusted completely, according to the White Leghorn.

That meant, Michiel Van Beusekom is to be trusted, according to Dirk Knopper.

Michiel found Mr. Postma at home. When he had read the note, he looked searchingly at Michiel.

"Do you know where the White Leghorn is?"

Michiel nodded.

"Is he in prison?"

"He escaped."

"Thank God. Where is he?"

Michiel looked his former schoolteacher straight in the eyes and said nothing.

"All right, what can I do for you?"

Michiel told his story and gave him the name of the traitor.

"We would like to hand him over to you," he concluded.

After a moment's thought, Postma agreed to receive the prisoner at the edge of the Dagdaler woods at half past seven the next evening.

"How? On foot?" Michiel asked.

"Yes."

"Don't you think he might escape and hide in the crowd?"

"By half past seven, it will be getting dark. There aren't many people in the streets by then. I shan't take the main road, and will only have to cross it to get to the station. There won't be many people there. Still, there is a risk. Perhaps you wouldn't mind coming too, so that we can take him between us?"

"O.K."

"Well, see you tomorrow."

———

Jack went on all fours with Michiel until they were clear of the saplings. Then he handed Michiel the pistol.

"If he tries to get away, just shoot," he said.

Michiel nodded, and tried his best to seem calm. Would he be able to shoot a man he had liked so much for so long? He made Van Hierden walk in front of him and kept the pistol under his coat. Once they were out of Jack's sight, Van Hierden turned around.

"Must we walk through the woods in single file like this? We used to have so many friendly walks together," he said reproachfully.

"Walk on," Michiel muttered.

But Ben Van Hierden did not walk on. He sat down on a tree trunk. Michiel took the pistol from under his coat and pointed it at Van Hierden's head.

"I'll shoot you," he said, but his voice did not sound very convincing.

"I don't believe you," Van Hierden said. "You can't shoot me. We have been friends for too long. Come on, sit down and let's have a talk."

"Get going, you," Michiel's voice trembled.

"Just listen, Michiel, try to understand me. I believe that the Nazi system in Germany is the best for our country and for the whole world. *You* don't have to agree, but some people honestly believe it, and I'm one of them. So, it's my duty to do all I can to help the Germans. Is that not my true obligation?"

"No," said Michiel. "Nobody is obliged to be a traitor to his country and his people. Willem Stomp was shot. Dirk's toes are broken."

"Every war has horrible incidents," Van Hierden argued. "I do not want these things to happen any more than you do. Do you think the Russians or the Americans are such fine people?"

"They are fighting for a just cause," Michiel said. "But I do not want to talk to you. Get up and walk on."

"What do you think the resistance will do to me, Michiel? The same as the Germans did to Dirk? They will torture me until I have told them everything they want to know, and then they will shoot me."

"That is what you deserve," Michiel said uncertainly. Would Mr. Postma be capable of doing such a thing he wondered . . . ? On the other hand, perhaps he had only imagined Uncle Ben to be a traitor.

"I will just walk off down this little path," Van Hierden said calmly. "You will tell them I escaped when a German patrol entered the wood. I promise, you will never see me again."

He got up and backed slowly away, not once taking his eyes off Michiel. Michiel stood there, pistol in hand and did not move. Could he fire on such a familiar face? He thought of his father and the Baroness, of Dirk and Jannechin. Would any of these people benefit from the death of Ben Van Hierden . . . ? Jack would be caught, Van Hierden knew the hideout, and Erica and he would be shot. But still he did not move. And his mother . . . his mother would receive a letter once more, perhaps two letters in one envelope, saying that her daughter and her son . . . She would clench her teeth and send Jochem into the resistance. The crazy idea of a boy of six in the resistance broke the spell. He pictured in his mind the dry eyes of his mother, and at that moment Van Hierden's smile turned into a false grin. Michiel leaped forward and pulled the trigger. The bullet hit nothing, but it sounded unusually loud in the still evening. Van Hierden instinctively raised his hands.

"And now, get going," Michiel ordered, "or the next one won't miss!"

The traitor realized that he had failed. Meekly he set off in the direction Michiel indicated. A short while later, they met Mr. Postma, who, worried by the sound of shooting, had started into the woods to find them.

"He tried to escape," Michiel explained.

Mr. Postma was wearing a raincoat with wide pockets. In the right-hand one he held a pistol. He walked up alongside Van Hierden and pushed the pistol through the material of his coat into the man's ribs.

"I'll shoot first and warn you afterward," he said.

Michiel walked on the other side of his ex-uncle. Nobody spoke. Twice they met people they knew, whom they greeted as casually as possible. They soon reached the station road and at once realized that something was wrong. The road looked different somehow. What was it?

"Munition containers," Mr. Postma whispered. Under the trees, about two hundred yards apart, stood five well-camouflaged wagons. They were closed on all sides, but there was no doubt about what they were.

"Are they dangerous?" Michiel asked.

"Very dangerous. A cigarette end could spell disaster." A moment later Michiel heard a buzzing in the distance.

"I think Rinus de Raadt is paying us a visit," he said. Mr. Postma stood still.

"You're right. A Spitfire. That's dangerous."

Michiel was not impressed. He had seen English fighters in action many times. The sound came nearer.

"We must hide," Mr. Postma said, and when Michiel did not move he added angrily, "Don't you understand? One bullet in one of those wagons and the whole village could blow up."

He pushed Van Hierden into a foxhole.

"You stay there or I'll shoot."

He jumped into the next hole and Michiel went into the one after that. Mr. Postma peered toward Van Hierden. A moment later, the airplane dived. They all ducked, but nothing happened. The fighter disappeared and Michiel started to climb out of the hole, but Mr. Postma signaled him to stay where he was.

"He may come back!" he shouted.

And so it happened. The pilot must have seen something suspicious. He banked sharply over the village and came back, parallel to the road, and flying lower than before. As the frightening roar came closer, Michiel and Mr. Postma drew in their heads. But Ben Van Hierden took his chance. He jumped out and, before Michiel or Mr. Postma spotted him, he was more than four yards away, zigzagging across the road. Mr. Postma wanted to shoot, but was afraid of hitting the munition wagons. It did not matter, anyway. The Spitfire opened fire and hit one of the wagons. There was an ear-deafening roar. The earth shook. Mr. Postma and Michiel crouched deeper into their holes. Two of the cars—the ones farthest away—exploded. Where they had stood there were now two enormous craters. A tree lay across the road. Three houses lay in ruins. Rubble was strewn everywhere.

When the roar of the explosions had died away, Mr. Postma and Michiel climbed white-faced out of their holes. Ben Van Hierden had disappeared—only fragments of his clothing gave evidence that he once existed. From all sides, people came running toward them to see if they needed help. Michiel wanted to go and talk to them, but Postma said, "Let's get out of here."

"Why? Van Hierden is dead now."

"Because of our weapons. If they search us, we are lost."

"You're right."

So they went their separate ways: Mr. Postma home, and Michiel to the hideout. He had to return the pistol to Jack and Dirk and to tell them what had happened. In spite of the shock, he felt relieved. Ben Van Hierden could do no more harm. But he also felt tired, exhausted by the strain, anxiety, and responsibility. When would this horrible war come to an end, he wondered.

Chapter 16

Five English tanks arrived in the village. The Van Beusekom family had started lunch. Mrs. Van Beusekom, who could see the street from where she sat, was the first to notice the strange-looking vehicles. They were less heavy than the German ones, more elegant, so to speak. In each turret a man could be seen from the waist upward. The British soldiers had light-colored jackets and their berets were pulled jauntily over one ear. Mrs. Van Beusekom leaped up and shouted louder than they had ever heard her, "The liberators!"

People began to pour out of the houses. They wore orange bands and carried red-white-and-blue flags.

They climbed on to the tanks and kissed the soldiers. Jews, escaped prisoners, and hidden pilots emerged from their hideouts. Everybody sang and danced and laughed for joy. There was not one German left in the village. The barracks were empty. The night before, they had pulled out and withdrawn over the river Yssel.

The resistance workers no longer needed to hide either. They wore orange bands around their arms with the letters H.F.—Home Forces—on them. Those who had been in the resistance for the longest were weary and modest. They simply tied up the necessary loose ends and left it at that. Those who had joined only within the last few weeks were full of talk about their own exploits. They amused themselves by revealing everyone who had been friendly with the Germans. Girls who had flirted with German soldiers were subjected to having their hair cut off. Male collaborators were put on the handlebars of motor bikes and driven through the whole village with their hands held high, and then were thrown into prison. Some had done no harm to anyone, but had simply been afraid. Schafter was also treated like this, though it was soon found to have been a big mistake. In fact, he had been hiding three Jews in his house all along. He was released once this was discovered and Michiel went to see him to say how sorry he was for misjudging him.

"You thought I had given away the Koppel-ferry

business; after all, we had talked about it that very morning," Schafter remarked.

"I'm very sorry about that, but you asked me so many questions. And everybody said you were always talking to the Germans . . . so everything looked as if . . ."

Schafter nodded.

"I've had these people in my house since 1942. After a while, I noticed that the Germans were getting suspicious. So I decided to play up to them. I helped them with a few little things, nothing important, of course. I never gave them information about anybody."

"Didn't you point out Bertus's house to them?"

"Good heavens, no!"

"Jannechin told me that you had been seen whispering to the Germans that day."

"Oh, you mean that? They asked me the way to Driekusmans Lane and of course I showed them— they could have found that out from any map of the village."

"However did you know that I had put that note in your letter box?" Michiel asked.

"Oh, that was my stowaways. We had made a small hole in the front door and when they heard someone walking over the gravel in the front garden, they looked out to see who was there. From their description I knew it must have been you. I had realized you suspected me because of the ferry."

"I see," said Michiel. "I'm sorry for being so suspicious. But you were rather inquisitive."

"That's just my nature." Schafter grinned.

"Did you mind terribly being exhibited like that just now?"

"Well, I was scared of falling off the motor bike, that was all. I knew they would soon find out the truth. You know who came to fetch me?"

"Yes, I saw you passing. It was Dries Grotedorst, wasn't it?"

"Exactly. They had hidden the motor bike under a haystack. They've made a lot of money during these past few years, that family. They were asking twelve new prewar sheets for one pound of butter, so they say."

"Well, not many people took advantage in this village," Michiel remarked.

"That's true. The farmers around here were honest and humane," Shafter admitted. "But not the Grotedorsts. Dries has been in the resistance for only twenty-two days, so short a time that he didn't even know that I have been in it for two and a half years. Oh well . . . at least he can drive a motor bike."

"And I had thought he was someone rather important in the resistance. The mistakes one can make . . . Thank goodness it's all over now."

"You're right. But how many people can really celebrate? The stowaways from my house are walking in the streets again after three years. Are they happy?

Perhaps they are, but they are the only members of their family to survive. Not a nice thought to start with."

Michiel thought of his father.

"You know how it feels," Schafter said.

"Yes, especially for my mother, it's not easy. Do you remember the two farmers' wives I took across the river on the ferry? They were a Mr. Kleerkoper and his son. Today, a passerby gave me a note saying that they were all right. They, too . . . " He did not finish his sentence.

"They say that out of the 250,000 Jews in the Netherlands, there are no more than 15,000 still alive," Schafter remarked.

"It's terrible."

Michiel went home. In spite of Schafter's gloomy words and in spite of his mother's sad eyes, Michiel felt joy rising inside him. After all, it was over. Hitler had been defeated and all the shooting, murder, and torture had come to an end. Dirk was back, safe and sound, with his parents. Jack was with his squadron and had written a long love letter, full of spelling mistakes, to Erica. Ferryman Van Dyk had died in a concentration camp, but Bertus was back home. There was no more hunger. They could all eat that marvelous corned beef, or whatever it was. The Allied soldiers lived in such luxury. Their casual sporty uniforms were much nicer than the stiff German ones. As they drove through the village in their funny little cars, called jeeps, they would joke with the girls and throw cigarettes and tins of food to those who were watching.

Life was becoming colorful again. Certainly you heard about death, but you also heard about people who had escaped it in many bizarre ways. In the towns, many people had died; but, odd though it might seem, some were healthier as a result of enforced diet restraint—they were rid of ulcers and other ailments because they had stopped overeating. Newspapers were in print again and one could even read them in the middle of the street! How different from the underground papers, which had been dangerous to possess! There was dancing and singing, leaping and jumping, crying and yelling. People could not get enough of rejoicing. They had been sad for five years. Now there was happiness because of the peace: peace after a war that would never, never happen again.

A few months later, the war with Japan had come to an end. The Americans had devised two horrifying, all-destructive atom bombs. One each had been dropped on Hiroshima and Nagasaki, wiping out all their men, women, and children, and laying waste the two Japanese cities. As a result, Japan had capitulated. The sorely damaged world could at last lick its wounds.

One summer evening, Michiel went for a stroll with Dirk. They walked slowly, as Dirk's right foot was in plaster. The surgeon at the hospital had broken his toes again and reset them, this time under anesthetic. If the operation was successful, they would treat his left foot as well. They hoped that Dirk would be able to walk normally again within a year. But for the moment he had to hobble along with a cane.

As they walked, they saw Gert Verkoren, an athletic-looking young man of about twenty-five, coming toward them.

"You see Gert there?"

"Yes, what about him?"

"He was the third man in the raid on the distribution office at Lowsand."

"The man you didn't betray?" Michiel asked admiringly. Dirk nodded. Gert came up to them.

"Hello, Gert."

"Hello, Dirk, Hello, Michiel." He stopped to have a chat.

"How is your foot doing, Dirk?"

"Fine. Next year I'll be running in the village sports."

"If it hadn't been for me, you would have been running this year," Gert said. "And you'd probably win. Well, I'm very grateful, you know. . . ."

"That's all right," Dirk said. "You had the luck and I didn't, that's all there was to it."

Modestly, he changed the subject. "Say, Gert, that's a fine shirt you're wearing."

"Nice, isn't it? My girl friend made it out of parachute silk. I once found a dead Boche wrapped in a parachute. Well, I didn't have much use for him, but parachute material is quite another matter, if you know what I mean."

Michiel's mouth dropped open, but he uttered no sound. Dirk rested his hand on his shoulder, as if to say, "Let me speak for you." Quite calmly, he said, "When was that?"

"Oh, just before our raid. After that, I went up north. It was only when I came back that I remembered that the parachute was waiting for me in the barn, under the chickenfood."

"Do you know, that. . . . ?"

"Do I know what?"

"Oh well, nothing. Let's get going. 'Bye, Gert."

"*Ciao*."

As they strolled on, Dirk said to Michiel in an apologetic tone, "There was no point in talking about it."

"You were right. It would do no good. There's only one thing that matters."

"And what's that?"

"That we'll never again fight *in* a war, only *against* a war."

"Quite so," said Dirk.

Many years have passed. Michiel is now forty-three. He has read the papers well and he knows that since that evening walk with Dirk there has been fighting in Indonesia, Yugoslavia, Hungary, Northern Ireland, China, Korea, Vietnam, Cambodia, the Congo, Algeria, Israel, Egypt, Syria, Jordan, Ecuador, the Dominican Republic, Cuba, Honduras, Mozambique, Biafra, Kashmir, Bangladesh, and many, many more countries.

Utrecht, January 1972.